The

"Beau is back, once again proving he is the alchemist of conflict as he continues to peel back the fingernails of human frailty and forces us to stare into the darkness found there."
—Tom Pitts, author of *101*

"Beau Johnson puts his subjects under the microscope. What we get is, yes, the truth, but more than that: we get an extreme close-up of the horrifically beautiful."
—Joe Clifford, author of *The One That Got Away*

"Set aside a few hours for this compelling collection. One story just isn't enough, and the next thing you know you'll be grumpy at work because you stayed up way past your bedtime."
—Paul Heatley, author of *Fatboy*

"Beau Johnson takes you to dark places and shines a light on the ugly things that happen there. *The Big Machine Eats* is the perfect follow-up to his debut *A Better Kind of Hate*."
—Marietta Miles, author of *May*

"These deliciously dark stories will stay with you long after you've read them. *The Big Machine Eats* is a gripping collection from a writer at the top of his game."
—Gary Duncan, author of *You're Not Supposed To Cry*

"Clearly the best collection you will read this year."
—Kevin Berg, author of *Daddy Monster*

"Beau Johnson has a way of luring you in with his sharp wit, discerning eye, and conversational voice. A brutal collection from a ferociously twisted mind."
—Sarah M. Chen, author of *Cleaning Up Finn*

THE BIG MACHINE EATS

BEAU JOHNSON

THE BIG
MACHINE EATS

STORIES

Down & Out Books
3959 Van Dyke Rd, Ste. 265
Lutz, FL 33558
www.DownAndOutBooks.com

Cover design by Zach McCain

ISBN: 1-948235-54-4
ISBN-13: 978-1-948235-54-9

for Dana

CONTENTS

PREFACE

Many stories populate this book. Some stand alone. Others connect. The one which do connect involve Bishop Rider and John Batista, a couple of characters from my first collection, *A Better Kind of Hate*. Truth be told, I have become quite fond of these two gentlemen. Bishop Rider is ex-police and at one time Batista and he had been partners. It isn't until Rider returns from Kuwait and finds that his sister and mother have been abducted and murdered that he becomes a man who is forced to change. Helped by Batista, even though John still wears the badge, Rider sets out to find the men responsible for destroying his life. In the process, Batista begins to understand what Rider has already figured out: you kill, you die. Simple as that.

What happens next?

These are their stories.

WHAT JULIE SAID

"Do you ever think about your mother when we fuck?"
That was Julie, all five feet two of her. She said shit like
that for the reaction mostly, and it took me time to figure
such things out. Something from her childhood I imagined, same reason she only wore black. Her hair lacked
any kind of polish as well, but really, what the hell did I
care? Head was head—fucking the same.

It got to me though, what she said, and I pulled out.
"Too much?" She coos, and attempts to lure me back. I
am sitting up by this point, on the edge of my bed, and
she has gone to caressing my back in long lazy strokes.
She is twenty-two, younger than me by three years, and I
tell her to knock the shit off—that some things are not
meant to be said. "I've struck a nerve, then?" I can feel
her smiling, of course, and know it's exactly what she
wants me to feel. I turn to her, my grill set, and then I
turn her round so she faces the wall. I don't last long, not
then, and I don't much care. What I am thinking about
is the question she asked and why it is still on my mind.

I shower, dress, and then drive to work. Later, going down on me, Julie discovers the growth. It's between the back part of my ball-sac and my inner right thigh. Small and protruding, it resembles a chocolate coloured Smurf. I touch it, trace it, and wonder how the fuck I could not have noticed it before. It scares me, it does, and more than I will ever let on.

I make a doctor's appointment and they tell me it will take up to three months. I say okay and thank you and go upstairs to see my dad. Wearing nothing but a towel, he is coming out of the washroom as I top the next-to-last stair. His chest is all sweaty; smooth, mounded, and thick. He shaves it as well, every little strand. "What's up, Champ?" he says and then winks. Champ is my name for the day, the one that began at dawn. Tomorrow it will be something different, either Sport or possibly Guy. It's never Adam, my real name, and I can't really say why. He loves me, he does—at least that's what I'm told. My Dad likes the gym and fast cars, but his friends I can do without. I believe they are anti-establishment, a choice that's never good.

"Could I talk to you about something?" He says sure, yeah, but the whole time he's rearranging his junk. Next, he flexes me a bicep, and then throws me an entire pose. As I turn away he calls after me, lets me know he was only messing around. I say okay, fine, just meet me downstairs. Downstairs he at least is wearing jeans. I notice they are new.

"Tell me." We are in the kitchen now, and both of us on stools. He is chewing the gum his doctor gave him, the stuff that has become his cigarettes. I say I think I might be sick—that I think I may need help. My dad tells

me he has just done my mother in the bathroom upstairs—that he has taken her from behind and I should
now be careful of the sink. I want to laugh at this, I do,
but I also want to cry. You cannot cry in front of dad,
however, as it wasn't the way things worked. "I'll be
okay." I say, and realize I'm close to being sick. Before I
can remove myself Dad stops me with his hand. "You
need to hit the gym more, Champ," he says. I concentrate on his gum. Chew. Chew. Move. Chew. Chew.
Move. "Toughen you up a bit. Then things like this,
whatever you were going to say, it tends to curb them.
Sound body, sound mind, right?" And then he taps the
side of his head in demonstration of his point. I want to
scream. I want to cry. And then I realize he is not the only
reason why. I am thinking of my mother; of my father
penetrating her cunt. Why am I thinking of this? And
then I think of Julie and the question she asked. It's then
the floodgates open, and the gorge that comes is huge. It
hits my father's feet, splashing, and I see the roast beef
I'd had for lunch resting between his toes. When I'm
done he looks at me and all I see is disgust. I tell him
that I'm sorry, that I will start to clean it up. Damn right
you will, he says; in fact, make sure you do it twice!

At my Uncle's funeral, Julie is beside me. Her hair is
red today, streaked with little lines of blue. This is new
for her, as it is usually black or brown. I compliment
her, telling her I think the colour looks nice. She tells me
to blow myself; that I can check it at the door. Whatever,
I say, and notice her ears and the extra piercings that are
there. She has twelve of them now, the biggest through
her tongue.

"Did you know him well?" I tell her yes, at one time,

but that it had been more than twenty years since I'd seen my father's twin. I see, she says, and I can tell she doesn't care. Hate comes next—that this is how she feels. We should be celebrating, she says, not mourning who and what they were. I say yeah, okay, I guess so, but I realize I'm fighting against everything I've been taught.

"What I *do* like," she says, and I can already hear it in her voice, "is all the rooms a place like this can have." I am disgusted and turned on at the very same time. Patient, Julie only looks back at me, her blue eyes wide. I say okay, but not here, my parents have raised me better than that. Suddenly my mother appears, all black and in the hat she only wears when special people die. She has been crying, I see, but her face remains the same. She is hard but beautiful, like marble cut to shine. I hug her, smell her—feel myself stir. What is wrong with me, I think, and then Julie and I are out back. She is on her knees and going, my back against the brick. Julie has always excelled at this, one of the primary reasons I've stayed. Done, she is up and in my ear, whispers *just enough salt*, and then, *boy-howdy is your mother missing out*. I almost scream, I do, but it would only give her the fuel she desires. "If you say so," is what I say instead, and then I take her hand. She doesn't smile, not at first, but as we make our way back in I can tell that things have changed. I try not to read too much into this, but really, once I start, I'm a man unable to stop.

At the doctor's office my pants are on the floor and his hands are on my junk. My doctor is wearing gloves. This makes me happy, but it's awkward all the same. "Cyst," he says matter of factly, that and nothing more. I stare at him as he takes off his gloves and proceeds to wash his hands. "Really nothing to worry about," he continues. "We'll have it biopsied, just to make sure, but I have seen this with many men your age. Not in the exact position, but we can clip it all the same. Anything else I can help you with, Adam?" I didn't realize what was going to happen, only that it was. It comes out gushing, like water through a damn. I tell him about my father, his voice, all his passive-aggressive shit; my mother, her face, and the love she always gave, and how I never thought about fucking her until Julie brought it up. I switch back to my father, now raging against the machine. I complain that he's told me things a son should never ever hear. I explain about his towel, how he stood there at the stairs, that I picture my mother against the sink, her hands on either side. I long to see her face, I say—what she looks like as my father thrusts away.

My doctor says nothing, not until I'm done. He then tells me about Freud and what I'm feeling is not as uncommon as I think. I say who the fuck is Freud and then his look becomes weird. "On some level, Adam, all men miss the womb," he says, "especially the one they're from." I call him a name, some name, whatever will stop the shit pouring from his mouth. He comes after me, running, mouthing words like unconsciousness, the levels and the like. I feel I have said too much, wish I could take portions of it back. Later, replaying it, I go over everything the doctor said in an attempt to find the truth, believing this would somehow allow me to understand how any of this occurred. It was then I realized what Julie had already figured out: I want to fuck my mother. Maybe I always have.

MY CONDOLENCES

When all is said and done, what I did is something I can live with. What I couldn't do is what I am having a hard time reconciling.

We had our first child, a boy, just months after we were married. The other two, boys as well, came later, two years between each of them. It's strange what having a child does to you, how it changes you. Not the inner you, but the new you, the facet of your personality that emerges once new priorities are set (kicking and screaming, oh my) and help shape you into the person you must now become. I wasn't always a parent, that's all I'm trying to say. It wasn't easy for me, either, there at the beginning, and Billy, my first-born, may have suffered because of this. I am a much better father now, tremendously more patient, and secretly I try to make it up to Bill, even after all these years.

Raising them was fun. Never a dull moment as they say. They were good boys, our boys, thoughtful and kind. Gentle, as well, just so we're clear. Jack was our extrovert, always his mother's clown. Bill, of course, was not the *total* opposite of Jack, not *quite* an introvert, but close, and to this day I remain convinced that this is solely because of my inadequacies, which, as stated, were present from the get-go—my unpreparedness, as it were, for this trek through the labyrinth we call parenthood.

Onin, our youngest, was a different animal altogether, neither Bill nor Jack, but falling somewhere in-between. Don't get me wrong, I loved him just as much as the other two, possibly more, and only because he came last: he would always be the baby. He was unique is all, landing not exactly *on* the fence but still within it, if you know what I'm trying to say. Onin didn't just march but *stomped* to the beat of his own drum. Not to say that he had been a mad or angry child, as stomping would imply. He was far from it; as I've said, it was just...well, let's just say that the world had never seen anyone quite like Onin.

Time passed, as time does. The boys started school, one after another, and continued to develop and grow at a rate that still amazes me when I think about it. I mean, from birth to five years old is just a miraculous process to behold, and I'm pretty sure I read in a *National Geographic* somewhere that we are the only species to do this. One more thing that separates us from the animals, I suppose. Anyway, the boys grew, time passed, and our lives became everything we wanted them to be. Looking back, I realize this might have had something to do with how it all played out. Our life was such a bright and shining star, it could have very easily blotted out the darkness awaiting us. Don't get me wrong, I am not trying to make excuses for my family—I am only trying to explain. The more I write, however, the more I see that this seems more about me than you. Please know this is not my intent; know that I am doing this in an attempt to offer any sort of closure the only way I can.

Onin was peculiar, yes, as I've said. My son: Mr. Unique. Tammy and I used to joke about how much of an old soul he was, as the saying goes. How deliberate and methodical he was at some things, like eating his peas at the dinner table, for instance (always in a line and one at a time), and at other times he was able to extract himself with nothing more than one of his quirky turns of phrase. When your four-year-old says, *"please refrain"* when he no longer wants to be tickled, you have to know your duck is different.

If anything, Onin proved himself anal, but someone who only practiced on occasion, if that makes any sense at all. He seemed to possess a pause button, leading me to believe he could turn this (his analness?) on and off at will—or not at will—I'll never really know, not for sure. And yes, I've often wondered if this was the beginning of Onin's personality disorder. I mean, it's not like he ever *seemed* like two different people as he grew. He still laughed the same, still cried the same, and got along with his brothers just as well as he ever had. If there *had* been two of them, then one most definitely deserved an Oscar.

He was nine or possibly ten when his mother and I caught him out behind the shed. I always hated that shed and wished we had never come to own it. It was one of those plastic jobbies, the ones that snapped together in promise of saving the environment. For the nine hundred dollars it cost me to help the planet, you'd think someone would've thrown in some wasp repellent free of charge; year after year our shed became home to more than our fair share of insects born to sting. Behind this shed is where we found Onin burning ants with a magnifying glass. No biggie, right? I had even done it as a child, remembering the act vividly, as a matter of fact. As my father told me, I illuminated Onin. And he understood, or so it seemed at the time, but all good sociopaths, as they say (and I now know), are excellent liars.

Was that the tip-off, then? To know we now housed a growing monster? Who knows? I sure don't. I only knew the moment passed and everything went back to being fine—our lives going on, the vacations continuing, Tammy opening her hair-dressing salon in the summer of 1996, and the boys proceeding to graduate. Boom. Boom. Boom.

Jack went on to become a doctor, specializing in oncology. He married in 2007 and has given us two beautiful granddaughters since then. Bill has yet to marry, choosing instead to concentrate on his craft. He is a writer, my Bill, and one who is faring quite well. I like his books (he has written three to date with another coming out in the fall) and find him especially good with the horror (or is it terror? I always confuse the two) aspects of what he writes. Personally, I love it when he describes the downfall of his villains, mostly when he has their intestines laying there like ropes upon the floor.

Onin? As you know, he became a sales representative right after college, working for Dunlop, one of the big golf companies. Three years later he'd found his way into their advertising department, an ad-man now, like that show with that guy, what's his name? Anyway, it was a fast life, full of all the vices born of man. When you think about it, it was a playground, really, albeit a twisted one all dressed up for show, so full of the things his damaged mind desired. He stayed on another year, continuing to do what he did until the FBI finally closed in.

(I will stop here for a moment to apologize. I will be apologizing later on, as well. The whole reason I began this exercise, really. I am choosing to stop now because of Onin—how it is he who remains at the center of this, even after all these years. He shouldn't be—that's what I'm trying to say. This should be about you and yours, and nothing more. It's natural, I suppose—what's happening here—but just because it involves him, does it mean it should revolve around him? I'm not sure. I don't think so. However, I seem unable to find another way to express what I am trying to convey. I hope you understand. As before and to this day, I am in no way defending or condoning what my son did to your families).

We never had any pets, except once, the kitten you heard about in my deposition. It was a tabby and Tammy found it on the side of the road while changing a flat. It had been wounded and was limping when she brought it to me. More so than us, it was the boys who nursed it back to health. Bill, Jack, and Onin taking their turns equally, each of them confirming our belief that we were, in fact, raising *good* boys, *respectful* boys. Weeks later, when the tabby went missing, we figured (as any sane person would, I don't care who you are) it no longer needed us. In hindsight...well, you know where I'm going. We had no proof, of course, and back then it would have never in a million years crossed our minds—as I've said before, our boys were kind boys, thoughtful boys.

And I know all sociopaths wear the mask, the one that hides their lack of remorse, but damn, when it's all said and done, *how* is a person to know?

You can't. I realize that now.

One last thing before I go. About a week before they arrested Onin, he phoned me. It had been awhile since we'd spoken, a month I'd say. I have gone over this conversation in my mind many times since and always find myself coming back to that one line of dialogue in particular, the one that started it all. On the phone, when I urged him to take care of himself in regard to the curfew and current events, Onin jokingly said this: *"I'm probably not the one you need to be worrying about, Dad."* It wasn't much, not at first, not until you coupled it with what we'd been discussing. I initially passed his comment off as just another weird turn of phrase, too—just the oddity of Onin we had come to know so well. But this time...as I told the officers...something persisted.

Was it his tone? His inflection?

Something I hadn't noticed in the *previous twenty-eight years?!*

I have no idea. I only know I was unable to let it lie, leading to the chain of events that brought me here, incarcerated for taking the life of my youngest son. And I know most of you don't call what I did murder, but it was. I was tried by my peers, proven guilty beyond a shadow of a doubt, and therefore, guilty as charged. Make no mistake—I took Onin's life as easily as I gave it. Did what had to be done, as my own father would have said. My father also said mad dogs have no place in the world, which pretty much equates to the same thing when you get right down to the guts of it. It *was* hard; that I will give you. The hardest thing I have ever done. It was something I took no pleasure in, just so we're clear, as I remember both the tremble in my hand and the blockage in my throat. I also remember thinking that this might very well be what suicide felt like just before the jump.

I am a man who believes there is no grey, especially when it comes to matters such as these. Tammy? Not so much. She has yet to visit me in the six years I have been here. Jack understands, as does Bill, even though I can tell it weighs heavily on them still. However, I stand as I must—would do it again if given the choice. Which, in a roundabout way, brings me back to the beginning of what I started here—that I have no reservations about what I did, about taking Onin's life. He was a serial killer, one who was killing your daughters, and it had to stop. What seems hard for me to accept is how the love for my boys blinded me as much as it did. Yes, at the end, the blinders came off—but what about Onin's *whole* life? I'm thinking I didn't raise my boys as objectively as I thought I had, and this is the part that gets me late at night as I sit and stare at these walls: that I was *supposed* to see the signs—me, Onin's *father*. That is what I continue to ask myself. And if there were other instances, ones I've yet to recollect. It haunts me. All of it. The faces of your children and the ones I feel I could have saved. As to Onin, I feel the fault lies with me alone. I do not say this lightly and pray it does not come off as trite. It has taken me a long time to gain the courage to write this…longer than I would've thought…because who, really, when you sit and *really* break it down, thinks their child will one day be capable of what mine has done.

As ever, I dream of preventing your loss.

P.S.

At a little after three on a Wednesday afternoon I hugged my son for the last time. Contrary to what the papers printed, Onin was unaware of what I planned to do. As the coroner's report attests to, I shot him in the back of the head at close range.

Before that, the only thing my boy ever knew was that his parents loved him.

Sincerely,
Jim Decanter

KNOCKOUT
A Bishop Rider Story

"You sure they're alive in there, Rider?" Billy Marwood.
Or as I called him, one-armed Billy. Decked head to toe
in woodland camo, he comes at me with a flashlight and
a grin that shows more gums than teeth.

I roll up the window, turn off the headlights, and exit
the van. "We don't have business anything comes to you
not needin' air, right?" Bill's grin grows wider at that,
his beard all curl and string and more like fishing wire
than anything. He needs a shower, too, but he always
needs a shower, and really, what the fuck do I care?

"Best get 'em in the barn then. Faster we get to work,
faster we get a taste." I try to ignore what he says, but I
can't, not since the window-licking gene in me failed to
activate when given the chance. I can't say the same for
the rest of the world, not if I'm being honest, but of the
three fat fucks tied up in the back of my van, you better
bet your ass I can.

Homework done, I followed each of them to the park
they hung out at. Dressed in sweats and hoodies, they sit

and smoke under a broken basketball net I'm certain they assumed they owned. Three darts deployed, all three down and bound in the back of the van, I go and change my name to Ahab. When none of them responds as I believe they should, I introduce their faces to the type of leather I've worn just special. I don't stomp, only mash, and only so they'd feel it once they'd woken up. A little selfish, sure, but much better than what they'd sprung on Alysha Adams, thirty-five, single mother of four.

"Knockout is what they call it, Bishop. Punks who walk up on unsuspecting victims and punch them in the face as hard as they can and then post the outcome with the hopes of it becoming viral." Batista looks down at the report he's spread out on the back of his trunk, then down at the dirt and stone about his shoes. What destroyed him is what happened afterward, when Ms. Adams succumbed to being knocked out, her head splitting open when it hit the curb. "Fuckers aren't even brave enough to take off their hoodies when they do it, either, Rider. Pieces of goddamn shit, all three." It was the children left behind, of course, the thing giving Batista the hardest time. He didn't need me to tell him that, though. What he did need is what I would always give, and the very reason he'd given me the call.

Hence, one-armed Billy. More so, his prize-winning pigs.

Prize-winning might be a bit of a stretch, though, as I've never been shown any type of hardware, and Billy, his stories mostly, they tended to change more often than his clothes. Not that I cared, not really, just so long as our goals remained the same. Our methods may be different, sure, and let's face it, Billy just liked the taste of his stock once they'd been fed human flesh, but I could live with that. What I can't live with is the very thing that brought me here.

"Fucking big ones this time, eh?" I agreed, more winded than I thought I'd be once I'd dragged the last one in. The biggest of the bunch, he lay there feigning sleep, the man's pants as ruined as they could get. Not that we could smell it, not with all the pig shit in the air, too.

"Maybe we should renegotiate our deal then? That what you're saying?" I get a laugh at that, and a blast of breath that reminds me of rot. Did I care? Sure. Was I going to say anything about it? No. Not this far in. Instead I grab a hatchet from the work bench and then offer Bill his. We turn and watch as six eyes light up and muffled screams reach a new octave behind the gags.

"Big pieces first this time," Bill says.

He didn't have to.

IN NEED OF A WIN
A Bishop Rider Story

I'm down to her next-to-last-finger when she finally breaks. A bruiser, she's more muscle than fat, most of her face obscured by stringy clumps of hair more red than black. I have to give her credit, too, for lasting the longest of all her counterparts in all the times I've chosen to go this route.

"Could have saved yourself a world of hurt here, Marta. Could have just given them up, and what happens next, it never has to occur."

It takes some doing, sure, but she eventually accepts all six fingers like a champ. She hurls twice, but after the third attempt, she comes to hold them down. She has shit herself by now. Pissed herself as well. She has wept. She has cursed. Screamed her goddamn bloody lungs out. I would have none of it, however, not one fucking bit; once you choose to involve a child, you lose all your goddamn rights.

When she begins to beg for release, it allows me to exchange my bolt cutters for a saw.

"Of markets and pigs then," I say. "I think we'll continue from there."

Culver has never been a kind city. Especially the east side. It holds the docks, the skids, and is routinely ignored. This happens by choice, and by men who would rather protect things they can see, not what they hear. I cannot change this. Not even if I tried. I can only change the things that I can.

"They run it out of two houses, each within a six-block radius. They alternate monthly between locations. Way I see it, it's a sit-and-wait type of play. No other choice." I hated the words coming from my mouth. Hated what I knew would happen as we gathered our intel.

Batista spits, slams his fist into the hood of his car. "It doesn't matter. No matter how many times we take guys like this out, no matter how many times, it's going to happen again." He wasn't wrong, the Detective as agitated as I've ever seen him. We stood in the shadow of a safe house, one of the smaller ones. Behind us, Culver slept, the city as infected now as it had been the day we began this operation Marta led us to—each as vulgar and godless as it gets.

"Means it might be time to send a different kind of message then. Maybe something the hardest of them won't be able to ignore."

Batista spits again. "You're goddamn right."

We hit them in transition, with seven girls ranging from the low teens to early twenties in the back of their van.

The driver eats most of a suppressor through his right cheek but the guy in the passenger seat we keep alive. It is he, pressed against the peep-hole, who gains us entry into the stage house he and the driver just emptied.

Inside are eight other men, from musclemen to cameramen to a guy who'd decided to linger. We move against them, each of them losing first cartilage and then bone. Rounded up, Batista positions their bodies in a row. After that, it doesn't take much, not with the right type of tool. The end result is eight heads, each about a foot apart, lined up on the fence out front.

Message sent, it wouldn't stop them, not as we hoped. But it might give a few of them pause. Not exactly what we were shooting for, no, but it at least gave Batista peace of mind. And more than the Detective cared to acknowledge, he'd needed the win.

THE ELEGANCE OF ABSOLUTES

I ask him about his wife and kids, and then whether he knew the truth about his father. I don't have to do this, not at all, but certain things in life are meant to be respected, manners being one of them. Marcus says yeah, big whoop, and I clarify what it is I mean to convey: it was more the *why* they took Big Jim's arms than the *how* that got us to the place we were now. "The symmetry I'm able to create from such a thing, this is what I wish to pass along." He'd given up his protests long ago, once he'd fully grasped the situation for what it was. I give him credit for that, I do, and exactly for the reasons you might think. Wrists and ankles bound, he's positioned as I want him, the table saw set to produce sandwich meat first, hard candy second.

"When you hired me, you said we'd be exclusive. Can we agree on that?"

Nothing this time. Not a peep. "For the sake of argument, I'll assume you do. I'm not so sure you understand the meaning of what you said, though. Oh, I'm sure you think you do, but once we factor in all I had to do in order to get us here, the dots, they fail to connect."

It meant an understanding was in order—that like his father, Marcus would soon see how a man is meant to regard his word. He would feel it was beneath him, sure, my words unworthy of his time, but the fact remained: it was he lying prone and I looking down.

Such things bring power into a different kind a light, one where men like Marcus find themselves blinded but bold, succumbing to the elegance of certain absolutes. "Take Mapone for example. I do him, the job done, and then you have your man do me. I get it. I do. I will even go one step further and sympathize as to how you might have come to rationalize what you set in motion. The thing you neglected to realize is what most people do: variables. They need to be treated far better than you would treat yourself, Marcus. You need to round all them bad boys up, you do, or at least give them a good old-fashioned what-for and question the possibility of something like this coming to pass. You do that, nothing like this comes to be. Since you couldn't be bothered, you failed not only to see me for what I am, but for what I have to be, especially in a business as particular as ours."

I continue, just me, Marcus only giving me his eyes. I tell him of my studies, my research, and how homework has always been my middle name. I explain how I compile what I find, weighing instance against instance, until I finally recognize his longevity for what it is and realize that it would be in my best interest to watch my back more diligently than I would have previously. "Common sense is what it comes down to. Occupational hazards and all that jazz."

He's a wall, like stone, but all this changes once I produce his wife's head. "This right here, this ten-or-so pounds, this is the symmetry I want you to reflect upon." It does the trick, destroying him, but I still wasn't done, not yet. I move closer, hover, and give him the one last look I assume he requires. I receive no thank-you for this, no "I appreciate the time you are granting me with the woman who helped me build my empire." Doesn't matter, not as it should, and I can honestly say I never really expected it to. What it does allow is for me to explain things from my new employer's perspective.

I enlighten him as to how Mapone works, and it feels as though I'm gushing. I'm not, though. I'm only wanting him to appreciate how certain things are meant to be seen. "More to the point, he offered me triple what you did, Marcus. On the condition you and I had a conversation before we got to the end of what this is."

Cat out of the bag, I give Marcus the truth: my resignation minus the two weeks' notice generally accompanying such an event. It brings a look I have seen before, but look or no look, communication is what's key. I reiterate that a man's word is his bond and that somewhere along the line he'd forgotten what this meant. He doesn't hear me, not as he should, so I take a step closer. Bending down, right into his ear, I again say my bit about the elegance of absolutes but add an addendum that, to be fair, would never receive the amount of time it required to shine—that unlike himself, I knew exactly what he was.

All told, it begged that age old question: did the apple fall far from the tree?

I didn't know, not for certain, but before I start the saw I give him my word I'd be sure to find out.

FREE FOOD AND BEAN BAGS

Big Ron's is a ghost town and Junior and I are in a booth at the back. I ask him to put his phone away. To just turn the fucking thing off. Not a day goes by I don't wish to have that piece of time back.

Junior looks up, his face as angular as ever, as angular as mine. He takes a swig of beer and then smiles the smile that tells me all the things I'd failed to teach him. "Sure, Pops. The floor is yours." Smart-ass. Him and his whole generation. Couldn't care less what the trophy they received for coming in last has done to hard work and what it's about. I wished he understood this—that my words would break through. As ever, it was not to be, not how I hoped.

Determined, I do as only a parent can do: I go on, delve deeper, and over-explain how men shot in the head can, in fact, come back from the dead.

* * *

Bob Moses was the man I failed to kill. Shot him point-blank in the back of the head only to have him resurface years later and take out the man who'd ordered the hit. The bullet I released managing to ride the shape of Moses's skull in an attempt at taking in the sights. Agree or disagree, it's the only scenario that made any type of sense. It jibed with the scar tissue, too, the majority of fence-work stretching from Bob's right temple to what remained of his left ear.

"As would I, Bob came back centered and with a plan. It involved a glass case, a man's son, and a python big enough to take a man down whole. You might think this impossible, men being the size they are. You go and break the shoulders, though, and Bingo: all men slide." I hoped this would do it—this, by far, the most fucked-up thing I'd ever heard done. "It means mistakes can be made. But we have to limit and learn from them. Especially when it comes to men like us and what we are paid to do." True. Junior's target a man by the name of Mapone. Dents in his forehead, Mapone was the type of garbage whose voice ran counter to how you thought it should. Top to fucking bottom, an all-around nasty piece of meat. "And I know you think you know it all, but you don't. Not as you should. But if you take anything from what I've been saying here, have it be this: two bullets will always prove better than one."

Did he listen? Fuck no. That would've been too easy. Mistake number one. Mistake number two derives directly from mistake number one and is the reason Junior comes to hang by his entrails in front of Big Ron's like a goddamn wind chime.

Kids, they never fucking learn.

* * *

Me, I'm a different breed. Old school. Take my lessons to heart and pride myself on never having made the same mistake twice. It's why I end up at Mapone's with a launcher strapped to my back and an aim that hasn't failed since I allowed a man to crawl back up from the grave.

As I tried to tell my boy: it's the little things.

SHIFT WORK
A Bishop Rider Story

It's because I catch him in the mouth on the upswing that the first piece of shit stays stuck to the wall. That he was considerably smaller than even the smallest of Asian men, well, I guess that might've had a little something to do with it as well. Like Chicklets, teeth launch and fall, more of them sliding down the front of what would never again resemble a jaw.

"The one in charge, Mapone, they call him The Goat," Batista says. The intel he's spread out before me is the stuff of goddamn nightmares. I'd heard of Mapone, the man coming from a long line of degenerates, each as vile as the next. That he was here, now, meant he'd been keeping tabs. Too bad for him. All told, too bad for them all. "These Asian boys setting up shop almost as soon as we remove Fontane from the hook. We have to go at them hard, Rider. Fuckers gonna think it's open season if we don't." This is where Batista is wrong, but not in the way most would think. I wanted to continue is all, which meant we'd need not just a little more intel, but new ordnance as well.

High-end, they were not shy. Had positioned themselves into fifteen acres on the outskirts of Brock. The residence held sixteen bedrooms, two pools, and the acts of men in the absence of god.

They worked in six-man shifts, six-man formation. The first guy, the one who eats my axe, I catch him coming from the shitter, wiping his hands. Quiet as I am, it brings forth two others, their mouths almost as loud as their guns.

I turn, dive, but feel shards of wood kiss the back of the Kevlar as I pull my own piece. I stay still, breathe shallow, and grant Jackie Chan a third eye the moment he sticks his head around to see. Before he hits the ground I'm up and diving through the archway. No one is there, his buddy smarter than I cared to believe. I chance the sofa, a big old red thing, and the second hole I create gives birth to a sound I have come to dream of. Around the couch, low, I put one more into the middle of him just to be sure. Done, I pick the smaller man up, hoping to use him as a shield.

It works almost instantly.

Two more bounding up the stairs, each as fat and bald as the bullets tagging the corpse coming toward them. I cut my losses, toss a frag grenade, Frick and Frack becoming as limbless as they were hairless in the time it takes me to spit. This leaves one, a man who is either smart and long gone or a man much like myself. I don't have to wait long to find out. Through the smoke and debris I see movement again, up from the stairs, and then there is gunfire until there is not.

I reload. My enemy does not.

Ten seconds. Twelve. I move fast, on the ground, making my way to the stairs. I find him to the left, near a Baby Grand. His throat, like the piano, is open to the floor.

I descend.

Wind my way down not one floor but two. Down a hallway that ends with a door I knew I would have to ruin. It's not the cameras or the cages that stoke my hate, however. No, it's the look at home in each of their eyes. It matches my sister's, there before she is ripped apart.

Rounded up, we meet Batista at the back entrance, the van still running. We don't say much, just load the van, both of us knowing the work yet to be done. I turn. Go back. And wait for the next shift to arrive. With them, hopefully, Mapone.

It doesn't take long. Headlights of two vehicles cut through the night not an hour later. I stand back from the windows, curtains just drawn. Gravel crunches, more, and then they turn onto the blacktop. Each SUV is as pitch as the souls of the men within, each as dark as the room in which I stand.

The grenade incident from earlier had been a contained scenario. What was to come next could never be.

Four bodies remove themselves from the lead vehicle. Bathed by headlights from behind, I am privy to their stance, that they regard themselves as untouchable—that they are business and nothing but. Like so many before them, they are wrong. Like so many before them, I would show them the reason why.

Mapone exits the second vehicle but only after the fifth man, his driver, has opened his door. He's as I expected, down most of an arm and pretty much half of his face. The parts that remain, red and raw, are intact but full of blisters and tissue you'd be hard-pressed to fix. Word was he took out someone's son. Hung the man outside a bar with his middles hanging from him like chum. Someone didn't take too kindly to this and went looking for Mapone with more than daises on their mind. The RPG that ripped through Mapone's residence did two things besides allowing Mapone to live: It got him gone and it got him scared.

Apparently, not scared enough.

"Let's go. Come on. Mov—"

And the night becomes light, the proximity mines I placed going off in tandem. The first four suits are eaten alive, burned, and propelled faster than one can blink. Half of one coming to rest inside the windshield of the second SUV. Mapone himself is still alive, already across the ground in an attempt to flee.

I exit the house and look for the fifth man, Mapone's driver. I needn't had worried. From above, I watch as he tries to talk through the blood flowing from his mouth. Or maybe he is only trying to breathe. Either way, he continues to do neither, not after I step on his face.

Low now, up beside Mapone. I grab him, turn him, and at first he thinks I am one of his men. This changes the moment I put him between my thighs. He looks up at me, I down at him. His ruined eye does nothing for me, remains as damaged as it had been before he chose to bring me into his life. It's his good eye I'm interested in. The one that continued to give him everything he craved. I tell him as much, but he doesn't listen, not even when I mention the prospect of his getting out of this alive. "Men like you need reminders. Things you can hear and feel and dwell upon. It makes you tangible, what I'm about to do. A walking, breathing lesson. If it helps, add it to the cages we removed those girls from."

Pleading comes next. Begging. Only when he sees the spoon in my hand does he finally go and scream.

Down and in, it comes out quite easy, optic nerves and all. Unlike bomb wires, they are fine enough to blow in the breeze, thin and dancing. Finished, I flick the spoon to the left. The eye flies, soars, and lands beside a tire. Despite retaining most of the lid, it does not blink.

I remove myself. Turn and leave. Mapone pawing at his face as only a one-armed man can.

For tonight, anyway, my shift was done.

A PATIENT MAN

My momma taught me to be a patient man. If anything, it's this I give her credit for. The rest? Well, she can suck a stick for all I care.

All told, it took four of them to hold me down but only one to make me scream.

Big Jim is what they called him. Head queer of cellblock nine. Bald fucker lived up to his name, too; I still don't sit right when the chair I choose is mostly made of wood. Eyeliner and all, he ate at the worst type of mean, and the whole place knew it. Cred was cred though, reason why he ruled the roost.

"You been duckin' me, I know." This is what he says to me as his bitches turn me round. We're in the laundry, the lot of us, and I'm up against the cold steel of a big industrial. "But Big Jim gets what Big Jim wants." The bull queer growled as well, like a goddamned animal in heat, which is pretty much apt now that I think about it. Why it'd been me—this I still don't know.

"You 'bout ready, boy?" What could I say? The man

was twice my size. Muscle as well as meat. Looking back, perhaps I should have hit the courtyard more, built myself up.

"I will kill you. You realize this." The last words I spoke until they un-wired my jaw. Finished, Big Jim's boys beat me to within an inch of what I called my life. I bled from everywhere it seemed, every orifice on fire.

"Fuck, Hollister! My wife gives up better head squattin' on the shitter!" This was after they took my teeth, once they'd been introduced to tile. Lucky to be alive? Sure. No doubt. Four months later I'm back in gen pop, but fortunate for me I'd made some new friends in the time it took to heal. Promises made ensured protection was kept. Three years down the line I'm a free man with a debt I was more than happy to oblige.

Debt paid, I'm free to look up that wife Big Jim mentioned.

Found, it's easy enough to keep tabs and bide my time. As I've mentioned, the one thing my momma got right in this life—this patience I exude. Fast forward eighteen months and word is Big Jim has managed early release.

After that, well, as they say—fish and barrels.

Eight in all and all stinky as fuck, I pay meth heads to take as many turns as they possibly can. Then I paid them to stand in line again. By the time they're done she needs a zipper to make her even close to being right.

Big Jim comes home early the next day, wondering why the missus hadn't been there at the fence to pick his ass up. He's all bothered, all holler, and then he freezes as he steps in the room and sees my face.

"She asked for you, Jim, she did," I don't raise my voice. Only state it matter-of-fact. Wanted him to figure it out for himself, you see, so it clicked and clacked and cemented into place. He rages instead, running at me, and I drop him before he's even half way to the chair. The report is thunderous, and for a moment I think I've gone deaf, but then there is a ringing, and I realize things will be alright. If not, no matter.

As I've said, I'm a patient man.

BIPOLAR BOWLER

Like that movie with Bill Murray, every day seemed the same. Better yet would be the Tom Cruise vehicle from last summer: *Live. Die. Repeat.* It was a good movie, better than most, and seeing how things have continued to play out, I have to go and pick my man Tom for the win. But it wasn't the same, not every day. The guy was the same, sure, and he always came in around a quarter past ten. Something was wrong with him, too, sick or something, his face just off. His shirt unbuttoned to expose a hairless chest, he wore beat-up jeans in need of a wash. Only once he's positioned does Mindy come and let me know.

"Dr. Kim? Your patient is ready to see you now."

From beneath my desk I grab the crowbar and make my way toward Exam Room 1. Mouth open, the man's upper body is tilted slightly back and down. He is wearing the sunglasses I provide to keep the light above their eyes to a respectable minimum. He doesn't flinch, doesn't acknowledge, and it seems as though time stands still until I bring the lead down and obliterate his face. I can no longer say this hasn't been affecting me. Not once my fingers begin to leak cheese.

Jenna asks, "You going into work today?" I look at her, there as she stands at the sink. Her hair is tight today, pulled into a tail. She stops what she's doing and repeats the question. *Why*, I think, *do I not go to work every day?* That's not how I respond though. Instead, I give her a kiss and a light squeeze to the bottom I bury myself in every chance I get.

It's as I leave that I begin to believe this causes everything to be right with the world again.

The next time Mindy tells me the guy is ready I go in with just my hands and karate chop away. By the time I'm done, I've torn into his mid-section completely, pulling parts of his flesh away in hunks. The process reminds me of prime rib and how my grandmother used to slow cook the meat for hours. He makes noises, sure, but the man never speaks as he succumbs. Done, I open the blinds and drop the majority of what remains to the street. I miss the dumpster as I always do, but other things are occupying my mind. Chief amongst them is the dark spot behind my left eye. It sings to me now, there as I try to Hefty-bag the place. I would object if not for the choice of song.

Ms. Spears would be proud.

* * *

"Have you lost weight?" We're in bed and the look Jenna gives me is one I have seen often of late. It speaks of sickness and disease, of faces just being off. I almost ask about Chris Redfield and Leon S. Kennedy, and why there must always be two and never just one. Instead, I smile the smile of champions and turn her round so she can no longer look me in the eye.

I tell myself to use my big boy words, and to remember Walter White.

It's how I bring the sexy back.

I try something different: approach him on the outside, catching him as he walks between the Freshco and defunct Blockbuster, which connects to the alley that leads to my office. It's as I suspect: no one cares. Not one person noticing as I start the chainsaw. Sidewalk painted red, I look down to the liquid leaking from the guy's head. It's like infection in there, or custard gone rogue. It excites and worries me, and I don't even attempt to pick up the pieces I create. Why bother? I mean, really, what would be the point? Would the Iceman and Goose do such a thing?

I am at least coherent enough to know that this is not a good sign. Not from a clinical point of view.

Question was: Did I still have "Top Gun" on tape?

"You're not eating, are you?" What she fails to tell me is where she'd been putting my pills. I couldn't blame her, though, not once I realized we'd been stuck on repeat. Maybe the guy with the unbuttoned shirt and dirty jeans was only attempting to change. Perhaps I should start thinking along those types of lines. Maybe I should attempt a conversation with the man and refrain from going full bore the moment we lock eyes.

Like I always tell Jenna: I ain't afraid of no ghosts.

And then I see them, all of Jenna's frozen dinners, there in the top of my office freezer, each one with a pill taped to the top of it.

"Dr. Kim?"

"Let me guess? My patient is ready to see me now?"

For all his scientologist mumbo-jumbo, I'm pretty sure Mr. Cruise would be alright with such an observation. Difference was I didn't need a couch to tell my girl how much I loved her. It created things, though, different types of scenarios and plans, causing me to admit that, yes, it was me who had become the one who knocked, and just because I shot Jesse James, it didn't make me Jesse James.

No, I had breakfast for that.

I'm much better now. Back to my old self. All because of Jenna, of course. So smart, that woman! So sane! I fought it at first, sure, who wouldn't, but the more I looked in the mirror, the more I remembered what I'd become—saw myself ripping metaphorical meat from metaphorical bones. Bipolar Bowler is what my Dad calls it: good at stuff one week, not so good the next. Makes sense, though, once you boil it down. It happening so soon after I proposed to Jenna, I mean. Talk about "Eyes Wide Shut," right? Anyway, I'm told the only thing left is the invites. They seemed to have fallen by the wayside during what we're calling my "sabbatical." Jenna agrees that this is understandable, but she also says that the time has come to correct our course. I share this view, I do, and it's because of this that the first invitation I fill out is addressed to Mr. Hunt and Guest. Mr. Maguire comes next, he and the girl he had from "hello." It's only when I come to Maverick that my hands begin to shake and Kenny Loggins floods my mind. I want to sing along but I dare not. Not while Jenna is looking. Instead I tell her to show me the money, show me the money, and then we share our little laugh.

It proves I have been, and always shall be, her friend.

ROAD TRIP
A Bishop Rider Story

Fontane is ruthless, feral, and reminds me of Toomey. Toomey being a goddamn piece of work in his own right. Hired by Marcel Abrum back in the day, he is brought in to take out Mick the Fish when Marcel decides to make a play. Toomey brings not only his own brand of carnage to the table, but a wood-chipper as well. Custom-made and portable, it's what he comes to be known for.

Until he runs into me.

That was then, however. Fontane, of course, being now.

"I'm not the bad guy here, Rider. I never have been. I'm only filling a void." Right. Tell yourself another one. But men like Fontane could see things no other way, evil and them as far from each other as they chose to get.

He pushes himself back from his desk. Thick, his face is more blockish than round. He attempts to come toward me, stopping when I re-raise the Glock. "If it wasn't me," he continues, big ringed hands now up and in front of the million-dollar suit. "It woulda been someone else. And fourteen, last time I checked, is looking more and more like eighteen every single day."

"Tick-tock," I say, and he gets my meaning as I begin to stand myself.

"Okay. Okay. But you have to realize the situation I was put in. Rock and a hard place and all that jazz."

I move forward, tired now, content with taking the long way if needed. Fontane reads the writing on the wall, the man right to the point by the time I have metal touching his forehead. "How do you think this all began? Who do you think showed those Abrum boys the ropes?" Another name from the past. To a time when a pair of brothers chose to destroy my life. "Their father made money at this far longer than you can possibly know."

Was it a ploy? A last-ditch effort to save his life? Maybe. Probably. I'm sure Fontane was counting on a version of some sort, the man believing himself a survivor. He wasn't though. Not where it counted. Reason number one was because he deserved the dirt. The other reason being Batista, and how the Detective has confirmed certain scenarios for me in the past.

"You're telling me there's a chance this man is still alive?"

"I can do better than that," Fontane says, and the smile on his face becomes a prideful one. "I can give you the name of the retirement home I send his percentage to."

The rage surfaces, my mind aflame with everything that could and should and might have been. I picture my mother. My sister. And then the men who took them from me.

I thought we had gotten them all. I figured there was no one left to get.

It seems I had figured wrong.

"Whoever it was, they hid their trail well. But yes, Jackie Abrum had been receiving, but no longer receives, a monthly stipend via Fontane Enterprises." Batista gives a little hand trigger as he says this, even though I had used a five-iron to take Fontane down. "I went back further. Missing persons from the fifties and sixties. Abrum Senior is on record as being questioned, twice in fact, but nothing ever stuck."

I finish with the pig-blade, put in back down into the side of my boot. "Doesn't need to stick. Not now. The connection between him and Fontane is all I needed to hear."

Batista grunts, swivels from his laptop to the computer on his left. "If I were a smart man, this is the point in time when I'd mention your lack of a valid driver's licence. If I were a smart man, I'd also mention that this plan, if it fails, is probably the one that shuts us down." He stops, stands, and makes his way to me. "But I also know you need to do this." Batista has been there from the beginning. Helped me destroy the men who'd destroyed my life, even after I'd turned in my badge. I can only hope he will be there to the end.

"The residence is out of state. Just inside Delaware. Should take you less than a day to get there." He adds the name of the place, Seasons, and admonishes me to please take care because the other residents there were nowhere near the likes of the man I was going to kill.

I promised nothing.

* * *

The sun is at my back, just up and offering its eye.

Seasons is more than a retirement home; it is also in-clined to extend independent housing for those able to afford as much. As it should be, so it was: Jackie Abrum residing on the far left side of the detached units sur-rounding the main building. Sparse, his bungalow was more like a bachelor's apartment than anything, but one that smelled of chemicals and age. Tethered to an IV stand and an oxygen machine, I find him in his bedroom, the curtains drawn. For a moment, I'm disappointed, but this changes when he opens his eyes, and I am granted something more. I don't know for sure, not at all, but I choose to believe he recognizes me. One frail hand paws at the oxygen mask but fails to complete the task.

"I never knew you existed," I say and approach from the left, coming toward him at an angle. "It probably means you thought you got away." He tries to protest, tries to move his head from side to side. Only when I produce the zippo do my ears hear what I had hoped they would. "Do me a favor when you get there, Jackie," I say and light the corner of the sheets down by my boots. "Say hello to your boys for me. Tell 'em Bishop Rider says hi."

I could have said more. Tons. But that's not what this was about. Everything in life has a price, good, bad, or how we envision evil.

In the end, it's how we choose to pay.

For men like Jackie Abrum, it's how they choose to beg.

NOT ALL HEROES WEAR CAPES
(Dave in Three Parts)

Pre-Dave (before but after)

I know where the bodies are buried. Well, the bones, anyway.

Ask me this question a year ago and I would have countered with, "Why, is the world about to end?" But even that would have gotten squat from me. This was pre-Dave, remember. A time when meat was still meat and I considered myself unscathed. Times change, though. People, too. And if this little meeting of the minds is about anything, it's about that.

We compile first. Always. Narrow down our selections based on family, social cues, popularity, and age. We do this to ensure our exposure is minimal and remains cursory at best. An exact science it is not, and very rarely is someone missed. What might surprise you is how soon a disappearance loses steam when there aren't any friends or family members to spur on the authorities. We tend to favor geeks, as well. Helps when padding the base. They tend to present as introverts more times than not, and this, this is where the fishing begins.

The twins are recon, with Bobby doing most of the driving. Me, I'm the face, the one who befriends and opens the door. This leaves Anita, our info gatherer, and Daddy Terry, who is mostly just a figurehead now, ever since the stroke put him in that chair.

By my count we have done it this way a total of seventeen times. How many times before I was grandfathered in I cannot say. If I were a betting man, rest assured, the word on the street would be lots. We'd make it last, too, the meat, until we found our next candidate and began the process all over again.

Dave changed this though, that dude somehow digging into the depths of me like nobody's business. It's silly, too, that such a meek and timid man opened me as he did. I mean, *years* I had been doing this. What made him so different from the others? I can't rightly say. Not without shaking my head. I want to say it involved everything I didn't know about him, but no, I can't buy that either.

Regardless, it happened. The dude never knowing what hit him until he's burning on the spit and screaming himself awake. It's a slow burn, too, his tits a kind of chicken slurry we collected and used as spread.

But before this...before this, I'm a beast. So on-point I won't even let this one guy, Cliff, I won't even let him watch the final episode of "Breaking Bad." What's one more night, right? Nope. Not the old me. Not even close. Same thing with the last book in the *Dark Tower* series. I could have given Darren the time to find out how King's epic ends, but no, why the fuck would I? I did give him a *there-are-other-worlds-than-these* salute as his time came to an end, though. It was nowhere near the likes of the *I-AM-THE-ONE-WHO-KNOCKS* salute I gave to Cliff, but hey, they can't all be winners. What this means is that I never cared. Not once before we got to the endgame a thousand times before.

Not once before my time with Dave.

What does that say about me? Again, I don't know. What I do know, however, is what we began this with: my knowing where the bodies are buried. More specifically, the bones. If it means I have to give up the twins, Daddy Terry, and Anita for the chance at righting things in the name of Dave, well then, so be it. I can think of nothing better, nothing finer.

And if I'm honest with myself, if I am, I'm pretty sure my man Dave would agree.

Dave (during)

There isn't a difference in the way we picked Dave and the way we picked any of the others. I think I just liked Dave more.

Chubby and short, recedingly meek, Dave was what society deems a nerd. His hygiene proved much better than others I have seen in their twenties, and I'm happy to express this. He wore Harry Potter frames and T-shirts solely representative of his favorite heroes. These shirts he wore under his work shirts, too, there at Mister Food.

An only child, Dave lost his parents to a car crash the night of the Millennium. When custody is given to an aunt on his father's side, he goes to live with her before he turns eight. Isn't until fifteen rolls around that the big C comes to change all that. Alone again, next comes foster care, and this is where some of Dave's time falls between the cracks.

We fill these cracks, yes, once he is chosen, of course, but now that I think about it, this might be the reason I'd taken such a shine to Dave. Because of what I *didn't* know. Made him more mysterious perhaps. Like how losing a mustache can utterly reconstitute a person's face. Either way, I introduce myself in the pickle isle, my main man Dave down upon his knees.

"You blocking the bread and butter there, friend?" Dave looks up, straightens his blue smock against the bulges as best he can. "Um, yes. Sorry, sir. B-Bick's or generic?"

"You think Bruce Wayne would ever use a name brand?" And I wink, pushing the message home. It helped that I could see the Bat logo through the back of his white work shirt, sure, but I'd already known coming in that Batman would play a role in what went down that day.

Dave smiles, his considerable mouth housing teeth so small and so large I'm almost caught off guard, even though I'm aware of the abnormality. Oligodontia. When six or more adult teeth fail to get the memo as to what the fuck is supposed to be going on. "The Bat, he wouldn't be caught dead using a n-name brand. He'd just go and create his own." The Bat. My word. But still, the shine had been taken, the stuff on paper and video paling in comparison to the real thing.

"That's what I've always liked about the guy," I say. "Always willing to take out the bigger villains when given the chance." That smile again, all those bitty teeth, like miniature, off-white Legos. He somehow reminded me of

56

Ryan, the first person I ever partook in and the toughest meat I ever cut. Dude had been a body builder, tight to the core. I learned, though.

Man, did I.

The next time I "bump into" Dave we're at his local comic book shop. Upon entering I'm hit with the smells of paper and dust and social inadequacy. "Pickle-man," Dave says, offering a hand as limp as I envisioned once the gap had been closed. He's wearing a hat today, one exclaiming, *Truckers Did It By The Mile*. Cute. Inaccurate, but cute. "What are the odds?"

If he only knew.

We spend one full year on candidates. One full year until we're prepared to strike. We need to know for sure, though. Wouldn't want anyone with too many ties—no immediate family, no one too popular.

Someone who wouldn't be missed.

His butt-munch smile, though…that hiccuppy laugh… and oh, how we discussed not only the Parker luck and how it could never be counted out, but also how Robin was maybe the greatest hero of all.

"The kid is wearing underwear to fight crime for crying out loud! What more does one need to see how committed he is?" I couldn't disagree. Not then. Certainly not now. I do wonder if it was this particular afternoon that our bond was forged, though. When hunter and prey became so close that the pain to come could do nothing but harm us both.

* * *

"You're sure your family won't mind?" Did he really want me to answer that? I kid, of course—but only because of how far we'd come and because of the pain it would cause. If anything, I had come to love Dave in my own weird way. It meant I would do anything to alleviate any and all pre-pain where I could.

The entire last year we'd been pretty much inseparable. Two dudes just doing their thing and fuck you very much. We went to comic-com. We went to movies, "Captain America: Winter Soldier" being Dave's top pick for the year. We even tried to get him a date, but poor Dave, no matter how hard one might try, some juggernauts remain immovable, prostitutes paid for or not.

"Hell, no, my family won't mind. If anything, they're hungry to meet you." As I'd been doing, I continued to salt the meat. Or what I thought was salting the meat. The real salting would come later, when Dave found himself upon the rack and golden brown.

First things first, though: time for the show.

"And this must be Dave! Colin has told us so much about you!" Anita always loved this part, said it was just like drama class all over again. She was the power number here, number One of Five. She looked good, too, despite her age, her abs the feature she took pride in most.

"Ah, there isn't really much to tell, M-Ma'am." He wasn't lying. The life he led consisted of work, comics, video games, repeat. Not the worst of lives, no, but nor was it the best. Getting to know Dave as I had, I tried to remedy this in many ways, but as the old dog and new tricks shtick goes, it ain't for introverts.

Dave stood amazed, took in what equates to a souped-up log cabin with all the fixins: animal heads stuffed on every wall, a fireplace spitting up sparks. Miles from nowhere, we are a property much like Camp Crystal Lake. Not as many hockey masks here, of course, not with the real ones hiding in plain sight. Me for an entire year, the other four for a few more hours or so.

We drink. We eat. We laugh. Dave in between the twins and everyone falling into their roles like no time at all had passed. Near dessert is when Daddy Terry decides it's time. *No harm, no foul,* his eyes say, *just salting the meat.* He's been sitting across from Dave the whole evening, his toupee much like roadkill and men who fail to listen. "Used to be stories of meat-eaters up in these here parts, Dave. Colin ever let you in on that particular crumb?" He throws Dave a wink as he says this—his way of usurping a lie that was more of a truth.

"No, Sir, he did not. He told me about that time you guys had a run-in with a grizzly, though. Shot its one paw clear off is what he said. Thing had a limp the whole time it tried to run away. Musta been pretty funny, seeing that."

"Sure was, Dave. The funniest part being it wasn't no bear. Was a man is what it was. One who got loose before the drugs took hold. A real screamer if I'm remembering my nights correctly." Dave laughs for a moment, for just a second, but as he looks around to each of us and sees that none of us is speaking, this is when he falls over into what would have been his chocolate pie.

Full disclosure: like meat in a slow cooker, my parts of Dave would be pulled.

* * *

He wakes up screaming because his skin has begun to slow bubble. Nothing coherent or anything, until we are given this: *but you were my friend!!!* Even that I might have misheard. Agony, she can be a fickle bitch. But I did *feel* something. Something I hadn't felt in quite some time. I liked him. I really did. From his nervous sniffles to the way he deep-tucked his shirts. I chalk it up to my getting on in years, my being closer to forty now than I am to thirty. Or maybe it's just my time spent doing this that's making me partial to the protein.

Either way, I find it unfair, considering the alternatives or not. It gives me food (ha-ha) for thought, though, as we take aim to begin this journey again. Maybe I'll go with someone not so nice this time. Maybe someone I would dare to hate.

For Dave, yes, I can at least do that.

Post-Dave (after the after)

After Dave comes Boyd, and Daddy Terry seems fine with this. With Anita's selection I mean. Never says boo, does Daddy Terry, just gives his wave of approval from his wheelchair and sends me and the twins off to begin. Me, I had lots to say. Tons. Like how I wanted something other than Dave this time around, someone I thought I should maybe try and hate. For truth, it felt like Dave deserved as much. For truth, it's because I'd come to like Dave so damn much.

"We will not deviate, Colin. We can't. We do, it's the

beginning of the end. No more circles. No more us. Be patient. Trust the process. Believe." Buncha horseshit, you ask me. But this is why Anita has always been the first and I have always been the second, Daddy Terry standing behind us all.

Nevertheless, it would prove our undoing. The last good meal the five of us would ever eat a man who believed Robin was the greatest hero of all and that *Lost* did, in fact, shit the bed there at the end. Agree or disagree, the man I spent a year grooming didn't care in the slightest, content in his own little world. This is what I loved most about Dave, I guess; that he was so absorbed in the mundane, he never once saw the monster clinging to his hip.

Not until it was too late.

Not until he began to burn.

But the new guy, Boyd, he was as similar to Dave as I was different from Anita. Not that Anita cared, not once she'd begun compiling data. Orphaned as well, Boyd Johnson was taller than Dave but just as heavy. Nothing morbid, mind you, just tits on top of tits.

I introduce myself as he rings up the remastered version of "The Last of Us." I'm already aware it's his favorite video game, and I'd come to see it as my way in. As ever, I'm right, an hour discussion involving certain apocalypses becoming my "Days of Futures Past" in the blink of an eye. Dude spit when he talked, too, with little bits of goop collecting in the corners of his mouth.

"The sequel is where they're gonna blow the doors off. They'll have to kill Joel to do it, yes, but what this will create for Ellie, this is what I'm excited for." He was not Dave. No. Not quite as humble nor as meek. But I still had a job to do, right? Of course I did. My heart wasn't in it, though. And I hate that I even have to admit such a thing. Admit it I do, though. I mean, is there any other choice?

So I begin to cut corners, failing to see the outcome I was backing us into. No biggie, I thought, when the time came I'd just make it up on the back end. The thing with salting meat though? It must be even when applied, and why our process, from selection to execution, totalled more than a year every single time.

You see where I'm going with this?

Yup, and it's the entire reason we are caught.

What can I say? I loved that little dude more than I thought I could. Dave becoming dearer to me even after we take him apart. He screamed, sure, and most of them do, but what stayed with me specifically were these five words: *but you were my friend.*

Gets me right here, even now, sitting here with you all. Makes me think I might be ready to take these next few steps. I'm not going to stand, though. I can't. I don't think it'd be right. Okay. Here goes.

Hello. My name is Colin.

You are not the problem. *I'm* the problem.

I wish you'd met Dave.

YOU HAD ONE JOB

"Tell me the truth: you didn't even recognize me at first, did you?" He didn't. I know he didn't. Only when I reintroduce myself does his double chin go and register me as someone who's back from the dead. "It's fine, though. All good. I don't much resemble the man you knew back then anyway."

True. Being chucked off an overpass and multiple surgeries will do that to a man.

"I know what you're thinking, too: how is it possible for one to survive something like that? I can't really say, Carl. Not to an accurate degree. Luck had more to do with it than anything—the handrail and my eyes locking eyes on instinct, I suppose. Either way, the way I bounced, I should be more than a distant memory."

True again. Instead, I break my face in six different places and pretty much as many ribs. I hold on, though, and end up in Tucson by the time the train stops. Once there I make contact with a cousin. Heal. Get work. Earn. All of a sudden handed my own crew, and then it's thirty years later and the big bug inside me decides to grow as many tumors as it has legs.

"This is the reason we sit across from each other, Carl. Why this colostomy bag and I have become the type of friends most can do without."

I tell him more, scads: how I thought about him a lot over the years. I include that I was at least smart enough to bury what happened and just got on with things. I concede that this was one of the hardest things I ever had to do in my life. "I wanted Marcel, as well, but it would seem he ran into his own type of jackpot. Man by the name of Rider, right? Marcel took a run at that man's family and lost, is what I heard. Was I heartbroken over this news, Carl? Sure. Of course. But it wasn't until you popped into view that fifty percent became my new favorite number."

The vein in the middle of his forehead led me to believe he understood the math. Hell, a man like him had to understand it the moment he woke up between the other two men sitting across from me. Mick and Tommy knew it all, too—every part with regard to the me and Carl of then and the me and Carl of now.

It means their timing would not be off. Not when it was meant to count.

"I bring this up because it's what I remember most as you and Marcel hoisted *me* up—that you and he were all about timing and how it would have to be just right to leave nothing of me behind. Again: how's that working out for you? Understandably, I've taken precautions so something like what happened to me, it won't be happening to you. And this is where men like you and I differ, Carl, and why you and Marcel ended up failing where someone like me will not."

It came down to commitment and how one pledged himself to such a thing. Maybe he agreed with me on this now, seeing how far into the black his life had come, but then again, maybe he did not. Back then, though— back then I think we'd both agree he fell squarely into the realm of could-not-give-a-shit. Either way, it's what put me and my boys in Jersey last night, the two men on either side of Carl integral to the dry run his youngest boy participated in.

I expected many things to come from my explaining this. I expected veins. I expected thrashing. I expected a bulging of the eyes. What I didn't expect was just how warm my spine became.

"Think of it this way: you'll have quite a bit to talk about once you and he find each other again. However, for that to happen you are going to have to leave the limo, Carl. You gonna make the boys drag you out, or are you gonna take this as you should?"

I want to say the rest was easy, and in a way, it was. Timing played a big part, too; yes, but that can be said of anything.

"The past is what we're witnessing here, Carl, and that whistle you hear is screaming exactly what you think it is. Mick, he's going to be the one who grabs you as Marcel grabbed me. Tommy will be a stand-in for you. They will each take an arm. They will each take a leg. The arc they create releasing upon three. You understand what this means, Carl? It means the circle you created is finally clos- ing. Problem is, my diagnosis not only brought us back together as it has, but it also allowed me to create one of my own.

"It's why I'm confident that that other boy of yours, he'll prove partial to trains as well."

A LESS-THAN-SEASONAL FALL

"Since I've retired, you are the third person to attempt this. I want you to know that. It means you are not as special as you think you are." I watch his head cock slightly upward as I say this, toward the chandelier above.

The images I have of him are multiple, from various angles and depths. He's even gone so far as to add a matching balaclava to his ensemble—one I myself had used many times before. Intent, I lean forward and await his next move. They usually take a few minutes doing this, trying their best to pinpoint the speakers and the cameras without drawing attention to what they're actually looking for. This one's a bit different, though, his one hand slowly effecting a crank as the other begins to salute. Makes me smile is what this does—the action performed by a man after my own heart to be sure.

I'm probably more on the nose with this than I should be, but hey, you don't get to see the bottom side of fifty in this particular profession without being able to envision all the sides an angle might represent. It's how you keep yourself from being ventilated. Or run out of a business that will always be less than kind.

Along with his finger, he goes one step better and removes his mask. I like this move. Actually, I can't help but admire it. His mug, however, would win him no medals. Not unless the judges in question were gone and made blind.

"You going to make me come find you, old man?" Bravado. Love it. Reminds me of me, back in the day.

He removes his gloves next, slides his hands through his matted hair and pulls it to the side. I don't answer, not yet, as I've found it best to let them stew. More fun that way. Not that my life had been boring since giving up the day job. Far from it. This here, Dude #3, he's just a by-product of what men like me create. I have become a prize is what this means, a notch upon a very particular belt.

Not that there's anything wrong with that.

Not if you possess the skill required.

I slide forward, lean more, and wrap my hand around the mic. "Better men have tried this. Again, it means you are no more special than the next. You think I am an emperor. I know you do. You believe I have no clothes." Did he even know to what I refer? Did it matter? Not really. I had come to enjoy this little game. As I've said: three times in as many years since giving up the gun. Since realizing someone has been talking, my goal has been to find out who and purolate certain bits of these guys back as a response. This had yet to happen, not as I'd like, so the garden out back continues to hold its color, even though we are this far into a less-than-seasonal fall.

"Funny you should bring up such a thing," Mr. Matted

Hair says, and poof, just like that, the game has changed.

He continues forward, his right hand sliding along the wood panelling as if he and it were in love. Was it his tone, then? The subtle uptick to his posture? Neither and both, I think. Too late, my stomach wakes me to the error of my ways. Too late, it registers the change of pressure in the room. Too late, I feel the lip of irony touch the back of my head as I have touched so many before.

"Some of the guys, they believed you were alive." It's not the man behind me who speaks, but the man on the screens before me. He's cockier now, his arms outstretched and walking oh-so-slowly toward the camera. "Once they did, I believe they tried what me and Frankie here are attempting to do now. Unlike them, we wanted to be heard from again. So unlike them, we thought to try this in pairs."

Not to be outdone, Frankie chimes in, the smile I never see as tight as the words it helps create. "Might mean it's *you* who isn't as special as they think they are."

To be fair, I liked retirement. I really, really did.

ALL OF US ALIKE

"We aren't the same anymore, none of us."

I can't say whether I believe her or not. The images I retain are as jumbled now as they were when I awoke. Memories I see through a fog or cloud that has set up residence inside my mind. I can remember most things, but with regard to what Ginny is saying, I haven't a clue. I still feel the same, perhaps a little colder, but nothing other than that.

Ginny—not Virginia—was the first person I met here. Aimless and alone, she found me by the docks. Until then I hadn't realized I was aimless and alone, not until she appeared and took my hand. "More will be coming," she says. Then, whispering, "Burnt offerings." The breeze responds to this, lifting her hair back and behind us: motion in the wind.

I did not know what to make of her statement. Not then, and certainly not now. I am coming closer, though, each day the fog a little less thick. She stays with me, Ginny, and we walk the circle, listening to mostly the same observations as the others. *Where is my mother?* they ask. *Where is my father? My husband? My son? My wife?* They inquire about their daughters, too, but their daughters, I must admit, are far from here as well.

We walk some more, upon long roads that always take us back to where we began, but sometimes there is change and we gather inside arenas. Not modern-day versions but the structures built in Roman times, when gladiators would fight and die with honour, their blood a treasured prize.

We fill the seats, all three thousand of us, and they continue to ask their questions as I secretly ask my own. "When another comes, I'm going to volunteer." I nod my response to her, knowing she will not be deterred. Here, Ginny is strong and more direct than I remember her being, which causes me to wonder if there is a history we have shared. I never ask her if she knows me, and she never tells me either way. Instead, we sit and we watch, listening as we do.

In the seats below us, a boy cries out in search of his mother. He is small, this boy, wearing jeans and a smile that no longer works. "What kind of father would do that?" Ginny asks. "How would one even come to think of that place for a child?" Then she turns away from me. For a long time we are silent, and only once do I really hear what she is trying to hide.

"Do you remember the last one?" I finally ask. She says she does and that this is the reason she's going to volunteer. Retribution, she says, and for the first time I witness the anger that possesses her. It is rage, really, and it contorts her face into a mask that I, for a second, cannot fully recognize. In response, one of her eyes falls loose. Dangling, it comes to rest low upon her cheek. Her anger is gone by the time this happens, replaced by the woman I have come to know. "I believe it is just," she says. "Each of them deserving what they have coming in the bargain." And then I move to help her with her eye. "Whoever is allowing this to take place," she continues, "they understand the truth for what it means— that in the aftermath, closure must always become the price that equals." I tell her okay, I can see some of what she is saying, but that I am still having a hard time of it myself—that my head remains unclear and sometimes I feel as though my body is a piece of meat on fire. She says it will come to me in time and I shouldn't try to rush it, that perhaps I am just not ready. I agree with her, and as we get up from the stands we find ourselves within a train station, all of us, the ones who died that day.

"Have we been here before?" I ask. Ginny says she doesn't know, not for sure, and so we begin to walk along the platform. The others follow, and the questions they continue to ask echo above and around us. Searching, the boy in jeans still cries, his shell in need of succour. Ginny can stand no more; she breaks from me and goes to the boy. On one knee, she holds the boy and strokes his melted head. "If you will have me," she says, "I will be your mother." The child agrees and they stand. Holding hands, they join me and we continue to walk.

The boy asks, "Do you think they will be caught?" Who, I respond, when I see that Ginny will not. He is referring to the people who got away, he tells us. What people, I think, but realize the answer lay trapped inside the fog of my mind. And do I want to know? That is perhaps the better question. Inwardly, I ask myself if it's

ALL OF US ALIKE

possible for a ghost to be afraid. "They will catch them, dear," Ginny declares. "And after they are caught, they will be tried, convicted, and then jailed. Not that it will matter, not once they find their way here." I attempt to ask her why, but Ginny only looks at me, her blue eyes shrunken and leaking but calm, always calm.

"When I get older I want to use the machine," the boy tells us. I do not have to ask what the child is talking about, the machine being the very one Ginny has told me she will volunteer for. It is the Righteous Machine, so named and made of wood. Housed in each arena we come to, it sits in the middle, asleep but on demand. Five sides, it has been made to hold all four limbs and the head, which sits atop. Slowly, we wind the machine until it can no longer be wound, the sound it produces being justice made whole.

This is the way it is done here, for us and him and them.

I am wondering about my wife when I come to realize that Ginny is not her. Rebecca is my wife's name, a woman of forty-two. I think of her without me, and then me apart from her. I have a child as well, a boy, and John-Edward then comes to mind. The fog is lifting, I say, and to no one but myself.

"Do you remember dying?" The boy asks as he slips his hand inside mine. The question shocks me, rocking me to the center of what I have become. *Dying*, I say, and the boy only nods, looking out and past the docks. I look up at Ginny, her eyes now proud and wet and new. She nods her head and suddenly I am back in Tower One, trapped between the rubble and the flame, between the metal and the glass. The screaming is heated, non-stop, and I am not the only one. I think it's what unites us, all of us who worked that day.

And then the tower *bends*, groaning—but it's not bending, only collapsing under the stress of its own incredible weight. The noise this produces draws screams from the ones unlucky enough to have survived the impact of the plane. It will be ending soon, those screams say—that and nothing more. Hurriedly, I scribble a note to my wife and son and place my love inside a wallet I hope they someday see.

I do this all as I approach the ledge, telling myself I have no other choice. Up on it, I realize what I am about to do, but deep down some part of me fights to carry on. Torn, I teeter on the brink but continue in my denial. Slowly, meaning locks into place and all at once a dark compartment opens inside my mind and lays waste to all I have ever held dear. My decision made, I begin to weep, and then lift my head as across from me I hear the South Tower buckle and then buckle again. The sound that comes is monstrous, but is nothing compared with what comes next. Stunned, I watch in horror as the building begins to bleed women and men alike. Like me, they are the ones who were barely hanging on. They look like me, I notice, as much as I resemble them. They are scared, frantic, and for the smallest moment I see it from another's perspective; I see the towers as they stand, wounded and dark. The smoke is dense, a shroud, like death made thick. I am lost within it, breathless, and then everything is made clear.

"Oh my God," I say and step in front of Ginny. "I jumped."

"Brad," she says, and places her hand upon my face.

She says I wasn't ready to see, that's all, and I wonder if this is true. "The means by which you arrived here...it was somewhat more traumatic than the rest." I thank her for the gesture, and then take her hand inside mine. I tell her that I love her, but not like I loved my wife. She pulled me from the darkness, I say, from the day that I awoke. She is Ginny-not-Virginia from four floors above, where she sat behind a desk in an office very much like my own.

"You would volunteer, then?" She asks, and I tell her that I will. But I also tell her this: I wish to wait my turn. I don't know his name, I say, only that he would have been in charge. It's him I want, I say—that only he will do.

"Lovely," she says. "Now we are the same. All of us alike."

COLLISION COURSE

He gets it: people see him as the bad guy. Thing is, he doesn't get it. Not really. The percentage he charges being well within the industry norm, nothing to shake a stick at, even if he says so himself. Salazar Mapone pays his boys handsomely. Way he looks at it: you want the best, you pay for the best. Anything less and you're just spinning tires.

What he's having a hard time reconciling is this entire last year. To begin, this kid comes right at him, gun already drawn and halfway to the table where Mapone is enjoying his dinner. Par for the course in his line of business, correct, but what Mapone is forced to do in retaliation is what really kicks things off.

Mapone has his men bind the kid to the business sign of the man who'd hired him, the boy's innards as swaying and slick as Christmas sausage before he's given a chance to beg. What Mapone doesn't envision is the over the top response to the message he'd been forced to create. The kid's father, under the cover of night, sends a rocket propelled grenade through a bay window in an attempt to do what his son could not. Unfortunate for Dad, Mapone escapes. He loses an eye in the process, yes, and part of an arm, but he survives nonetheless. Never one to accept stupidity as a way of life, it gets Mapone moving and the fuck out of Dodge. If a man would go to such lengths, he thinks, really, what choice do I have?

Planning to start over, he lands in Culver, a city he's had business in before. He and his new crew set things up, beginning a start-up involving girls who needed a job even though Mapone may have to remind them of this from time to time. Four months on and his year of discontent takes its most drastic turn yet. He's ambushed. And not in the good way.

The men in front of him exit their vehicle before Chen and Mapone exit theirs. They are dismantled as explosions rock the front of the residence they'd been filming in. The blowback rips Mapone's men apart, any remaining pieces coming down around him like a type of chunky rain. On his stomach and crawling, the heat is intense, the night now like day, but Mapone continues to do what he has always done best: he survives.

Until he is grabbed from behind.

Mapone at first thinks it's his driver. This is not the case. He'd like to say otherwise but his head being scissor-locked between a man's thighs goes a long way to opposing this.

Dark hair greets him. Then stubble. A look that said more than he cared to think about.

The man talks. Mapone listens.

The last thing Mapone ever sees being a spoon as the man goes and removes his last working eye.

He screams. He remembers screaming. Feeling as though he'd never be able to stop. But stop he does. And then Mapone regroups. Plays the part this man wished him to play. But he was no man's puppet. Never had been. Never fucking would be. A business man, he has only provided services and employment in exchange for the betterment of all parties involved. If he'd been forced to work outside the lines to achieve this, so be it. It's how most business models worked once you've read between the lines.

However, it's a fuck-nugget not much taller than his chest which allows Mapone to smile for the first time in months. His year of hell taking an unexpected, out of the blue turn.

No bells accompanied this. No whistles.

Just a man by the name of Alexander Paine.

Disgruntled, he comes from the very same camp of the man who blinded Mapone. Alex not only gives Mapone this man's name but all the names of the men he'd surrounded himself with.

"Sounds like a buncha Nancys seeing themselves as some sorta fucking super team. Tell me I'm wrong." Alexander can't, and the more Mapone listens the more his sockets begin to itch; the more he wants to stick his fingers in and scratch.

John Batista is a Detective, he's told, and the man who approaches Alexander first. This occurs because the man sitting on the other side of Mapone's desk witnesses this Detective, and the man whose life Mapone planned on ending, chop another man into pieces. Abrum was this man's name, his body transformed into quarters and not much more. Abrum who intruded upon a life he

79

shouldn't have.

"Boo-fucking-hoo. It's been twenty goddamn years, get the fuck over it!" There is a tremble in Alex's voice as he says this, and the anger that comes, Mapone can tell it is far from new. But the man they were discussing, he does not "get over it." In fact, he doubles down, onward and forward, he and his little posse going through men like Mapone like it was nobody's goddamn business.

What changes things is the aforementioned Nancy-boy raging in front of him. For minutes Alex goes on, lamenting about how he has never been treated right; that they never did or have. Saying it has all been quite, quite unfair. Never one to look a gift horse in the mouth, Mapone plays things as he believes he should and welcomes the opportunity, reaching out and offering his hand. It doesn't take much after that. Time, mostly. And set up—calls to get him some new muscle to help with the type of retribution he planned on creating.

Which brings us to the here and now, to the present and accounted for, when the door to Mapone's office opens and he hears them bring him in. Although he tries, Mapone can't help himself. The spaces in his face which used to hold eyes no longer warm but itching and furnace-like.

He clears his throat. He stands.

"Bishop Rider," he says. "At last."

OLD GHOSTS
A Bishop Rider Story

Letting Mapone live had been a mistake. I know that now.

I intended to leave a message—a living, breathing re-minder of what could and should happen to men who hold themselves above. It worked for a while, sure, his nose as clean and empty as the eye sockets on his face. But it couldn't last, not with a core as dark as his. I could take credit for the eye on the right, but not the one on the left—a man as angry as I had beat me to that little arrangement first.

Leaving both that man and that city, Mapone ends up in Culver. Moreover, Brock. On the outskirts of each, he and his men set up shop on fifteen acres, the type of mer-chandise they planned on selling the stuff of goddamn nightmares.

Batista and I, we scope them out, plan our play, and by night's end we remove the girls as easily as I removed Mapone's last working eye. Screaming and writhing, I leave him on the blacktop, his only arm pawing at his face as only a one-armed man can.

All good. Message sent and in the days to come, received.

Or so I thought.

"Looks like your little pep talk didn't quite take, Rider. Looks like this piece of shit has gone and hired himself a nasty breed of help." Batista was correct, but only up to a point. The help was new, true, but the blood behind the faces Mapone now employed was as old and as evil as it came.

The Aryan race had moved to Culver, it seemed.

For the first time in years I allowed myself to smile.

The smile didn't last long. The entire situation a setup, yours truly being the entire reason why.

"I wish I could see the look on your face. I really do. But I'm confident the noises you produce will do wonders for the pictures my mind will create." Mapone. Nut Job 101. A big man with a voice higher than it should be and a face that could only be classed as holding a little more than half of the features it'd been born with.

Tight quarters, dimly lit, he stood to the left of me, his "eyeline" down about my boots. Rounding out the office stood three other men, one big, two small. Unlike Mapone, they did not wear suits. If anything, they were stereotypical thugs, each of them shaved to the wood. In the biggest one's hand hung an axe, the handle painted red.

It was one of the smaller men who drew most of my attention, though. Something familiar about him from the get-go. But this is when the bigger Nazi goes to work, lunges, and puts the aforementioned axe up and under my right knee. The pain is immediate, a monster, and

82

how I have come to envision the upper levels of hell. Clear through, the axe continues on, and suddenly I drop, the leg of the chair I'm tied to buckling in the process. I'm on my side, on the floor, the bottom half of my leg now inches from my eyes.

I have time to think two things: It's over, and this is where it ends.

Life, however, she had other plans. Unfortunately, the lube she sometimes used, it was nowhere to be seen.

For truth, I pegged Mapone at running his mouth until he ran out of things to say. After that, well, come what may. That I lost the leg so soon after they tied me to the chair meant someone had come to see things the way I saw things. We were opposites, sure, but hate plays slave to no one, justified or otherwise.

What I didn't figure on was the little guy. Not when he moved to shield me, nor when he pulled his piece and put the other two skinheads down.

"What the fuck is going on?!" Mapone yells. "Who the fuck's shooting? Conrad? Is he dead? IS RIDER DEAD?!"

"Fat chance," the kid says, and gives Mapone his turn at the wheel, delivering an ending that should have been mine.

Back to me, the kid takes off his belt and hunkers down. Tourniquet on, he unties my hands and helps me sit up.

"This has been a long time coming, Mr. Rider. Longer than you probably know. I want you to know I never blamed you. Not for any of it."

I look at him again, his face familiar but at the same time, not. I wasn't one to play games, though, whether he'd saved my life or not.

"You're going to spit it out soon then, I hope," I say.

He did. And as he did, I knew. I fucking knew.

"My name's Jeramiah Abrum. I believe you knew my father."

I look at him, stare at him, take in his beady little eyes. They are black like pools, black like tar. He smiles, says it's okay, and then, as if on cue, all of it fades away.

I awaken in the back of a car, the kid behind the wheel. Darkness has enveloped us. To my left, a partial moon. I wanted to tell him he had to be kidding—what were the fucking odds? My ruined stump of a knee seemed to have other things on its mind.

But still, Abrum. The man who had destroyed me, a man I eventually destroyed. I had help, sure, and if memory serves, Batista did the honors that day, the pieces of Abrum that wouldn't fit into the wheelbarrow over-flowing onto the stage.

"I never blamed you, as I said. I know my father was not a good man. He got your mother and your sister killed. I know he deserved everything you ended up do-ing to him." I didn't argue. Mainly because he was right. More so because of the pain.

"If you'll let me, I can help you. Like I'm going to help you now. I know I don't have to. I know I was just a kid. But what you do, Mr. Rider…I believe it's a thing that needs to continue."

Six days later I lay awake in a private facility with a

leg that looks more bionic than prosthetic. A year after that, Batista and I are back to doing what we have always done best. But now we had a benefactor and an influx of cash that allowed us to stay a step ahead. What it really came down to was this: I'd been mistaking fate for coincidence.

I never would again.

MAKING UP FOR LOST TIME
A Bishop Rider Story

For his eighty-six years, Mantooth appears stronger than he is. Veins on his forearms like cables. A chest that could still be classed as barrel. None of it mattered. Not once we began. Four teeth falling from his mouth and we're halfway to the place I want us to be.

"You're going to tell me if there were more of you, Father. More than just Bobby and you. You tell me that and your ability to chew holds a much better chance of staying intact."

Cheap tent or not, he folds, admitting to everything that had been speculation up until the point where Bobby LeBec decides a boy no older than ten deserved the very same thing the priest had done to him.

Bleeding, repentant, the old man tries his best to wrap himself around my knees. He pleads. He begs. He causes me to rethink my offer of allowing him to live.

"Things are wrong upon this world," he says, his hands finally realizing that my right leg was not as whole as it appeared. "Things are not right within me."

"You don't say," and I'm already past the point of no return before I register his screams. He ends up beneath the majority of my boot, his jaw and the pew he ends up against a greyish-pink mush by the time I realize his skull has become something less than bone.

Batista was right: age would never be anything but a number.

"The prosthetic works fine. No worries," I tell Batista. I needed to get it out of the way quickly. If I didn't, there was no way of telling how far Batista would try and take things. Not that I could blame him, the man only acting the way nature made him.

"Your balance is fine, then? No real problems with speed?" I look over at him. He's thinner now. Too thin, in fact. As if he knows what I'm thinking, he readjusts his shirt, then does it again, ending with a hand that travels through a beard that's no longer there. I've said it before, and I'll say it again: Textbook and Batista, they are one and the same.

"It's been a year, John. The leg works. It gets it done. Can we just get on with it?" I lost the lower part of my right leg more than a year ago to an axe and a man who no longer breathes. Where I see this as time lost from cleaning up walking, talking garbage, Batista sees it as something else. We'd had the same difference of opinion years ago, when we first started out. But Batista finally came around to my way of thinking, which is exactly what I hoped would happen here.

"Fine," he says, but the face he gives me says he wished to say more. Wonder of wonders, he doesn't, and almost like that we are back to saving the world the only way we know how: one shit-stain at a time.

Overweight, wearing an orange track suit past the point of structural integrity, Bobby LeBec sits on the edge of his bed, blood gushing from his mouth. The fabric of the track suit absorbs most of the liquid, accentuating cracks and crevices that have been years in the making. I raise the hammer again and LeBec screams, holding up his hands to ward off the coming blow.

"There were others," he cries. "I lied. I LIED!"

Now we were getting somewhere.

I just hoped we weren't too late.

But we were too late. Only two of the six monsters were still alive. Three had been taken by cancer, another while driving under the influence.

"Three of the four died hard, Rider. If anything, we can at least take solace in that." It wasn't enough. Would never *be* enough. Batista knew as much, believed as much, but has always been a glass-half-full type of guy. Saying such a thing might suggest I am the opposite, but this is not the case. More to the point: the glass, in my world, it fails to exist.

None of this changes what Batista does, how he roots out the remaining two, the pair of them still holding ties to the church. A little more digging and he sets them and me on a collision course—a course that their wheelchairs would have a hard time saving them from.

* * *

The thinner one protests the entire way to the edge of the building. Over and gone, his screams continue, trailing off as I turn my attention to his buddy, this other "man of God." He's trembling, covered in liver spots, trying with all his might to remove himself from the chair. I slide behind him, release the brakes, and move us to the edge.

I remind him of the lives he touched. I remind him of the lives he destroyed.

I repeat it was time to fly.

KEEKO AND MEAT SLEEVES
A Bishop Rider Story

The knuckle-dragger goes by Meat Sleeves. Tore a man's skin up and off his forearm for this moniker to stick. Bull-nosed, with loops in his ears, he's a bouncer and right fuck-of-a-cunt if I'm to believe what I've heard.

"Not tonight, fella," he says, his arms remaining folded, his black-rimmed eyes back to dead ahead. "I can tell yer trouble just by lookin' atcha." Smart. This might go easier than expected.

"Just a location, big man. That's all I need. Stomping ground for a guy you used to know. Alexander Paine." He's good, sure, but not that good. "We can do this one of two ways then, Jerry. You tell me what I want to know and I leave this fine establishment, or—and this is the door I'm hoping you don't pick—I beat it out of you and you tell me anyway. Five seconds, big man. It's all the time I have."

Nice speech. Been practicing it for days. What I should have been doing was watching my flank.

From behind I'm hit hard, right in the middle of my

91

back. Keeko Reyes. Meat Sleeves's partner in crime.

And me without my hat.

"I think I've found him, Rider," Batista says. He was on about Alexander, a man who'd betrayed us both. Process of elimination was what it came down to, and there'd been no getting around it. It explained how Mapone and his men had found me, and how this dovetailed with my losing part of a leg.

"You sure this time?" We'd had false starts before, one involving Alex's mother and her death a few years back. No luck then, however. No good-boy son coming home to say goodbye.

"As sure as I've ever been. Routine traffic stop in Brock. Means the man is either nearby or he's fled because of the ticket. I say we check it out."

And so we did.

Here, now, I'm getting my ass handed to me in front of velvet ropes because I failed to check my blind spot.

"Now what was that part about—"

I don't have the patience. I'm wet. I'm cold. And now my back feels like it's been stepped on by a horse. I reach inside my coat and bring the hammer up claw-first into the underside of Meat Sleeves's jaw. It brings a *thunk*, only thicker, and for the first time tonight I get his undivided attention. Meat Sleeves is grabbing at the hammer, so I let it go and turn to the smaller man with the intent of making it quick. No such luck. I'm too old, too slow, and I know the fight is his after the first two punches. He emphasizes this when he blocks my turn and doubles back with another three blows to my right kidney. Down

I go, onto a knee, but then his attention is diverted when the doors to the club open and screams erupt as two throwbacks to the eighties observe the hardware Meat Sleeves is trying to extract from his jaw.

I take the moment.

Keeko screams, punches at my hand, punches again, but I don't let go until I feel his testicles change into something less round. It puts him down, onto the ground in a fetal position, so I grab his legs, lift, and spin him around. Two turns in and a face full of brick becomes his next-to-last meal. I want to be sure, to give it another go, but I can't. I'm too damn tired. Too damn old.

I lurch back to Meat Sleeves and hunker down. "I remove it, you most likely die. You tell me what I want to hear and you'll never see me again."

He had to use a pencil, but still. Smart man.

Heavier than I remember, wearing that same old flak jacket, Alex takes off the moment he sees me. I don't expect anything less. You do the type of thing he did, it shows you were not so human to begin with.

But he did help us a lot over the years. More times than I could possibly count. It all started the night he didn't give us up; the night Batista and I finally took Abrum down. That was then, however. This is now.

Ball cap pulled down hard, Alex runs all-out for the corner, trying his best to get himself to the second-floor stairs of the Motel he'd been staying at. Batista takes him out coming around the bend with a blade to the gut. Alex halts, holds on, but the Detective would have none of it, electing instead to make the blade smile. One move

KEEKO AND MEAT SLEEVES

more and Alex is gone, over the railing and down.

By the time I get to him most of his guts have spilled out. He continues to try, but no, they will not go back in.

I ask him the question I'd been wondering about for years.

He stops, looks up. "Really? Now?"

"Good a time as any."

He struggles to talk through the pain. "You didn't care. Not you or Batista. Not if I lived or died. Just so long as we did what you wanted done."

The anger sets in as I walk away, toward the van. I get in, back up, stop, and get back out. I approach him again, bend down, and rope a length of his intestines around my hand.

"Was never about us, Alex. Not really. You say we didn't care. I say, who cares about you now?"

Tying his entrails to the hitch, I ignore his response. I was done. It was over. There were too many people we had failed to save. Too many people who needed to pay.

I hit the gas.

Time to go home.

I should have known. That's what I think of most now, whenever Alex comes to mind. I couldn't have known, though. No one could. Still doesn't stop me from running hot more often than not.

The second time Alex worked with us he took two in the chest. The Kevlar stops one completely but the other bullet makes it through. By a quarter-inch, sure, but enough to open Alex's eyes. Why they weren't open already—his having watched Batista and me hack a man to pieces two months prior—I still don't understand.

Batista patched him up, sent him on his way. "Don't know if bringing Alex into this was such a good idea, Bishop," Batista said at the time. "Second time out and we're already to here?"

"Pretty sure it woke him up," I told him. "If it didn't, he's a big boy; he can find the door." I didn't care either way. If he stayed, he stayed; if he left, so be it. It wasn't the point, the job being the only thing that was. Then, as well as now.

Batista grunted. "You're never going to change, are you?" An old one of his. An old one, sure, but a good one.

"Now where would the fun be in that?" I answered.

Long story short: Alex watches a certain sequence of events go down, doing so in secret behind a set of barroom doors. Once Batista and I leave the scene he comes out of hiding to do what is anyone's guess. Me, I'd have hightailed it the fuck out of Dodge. You see two men stack parts of another man into a wheelbarrow on a stage, you have to acknowledge the world you're looking at for what it is: Hell. Plain and simple. Leave your children at the goddamn door.

After that, he's taken into custody and ultimately cleared. However, while he's in the station he recognizes Batista but keeps his mouth shut. Later, the Detective and I agree our best interest would be to keep the kid close. "It's because I recognized you at the precinct and didn't say shit about what you two did, right?" Attitude as well as brains. Christ, I should have seen it all the way back then.

"That's right, junior," Batista says, and I can already hear it in his voice.

If I had known then what I know now I would have ended it right there, in a parking lot that since has become a Denny's. Boom. Bullet to the head. Alexander Paine no more. But it's not the way things work, not in the world I live in. When your life is devoid of light and rage is all you have, you tend to take the things you're given and hope the choice you're making is correct. Doesn't matter if the fingers gripping you are ripping at your flesh. It's all darkness by the time we get to the end, anyway. You either embrace this and rise above or become like Alex, a man more concerned with his insides being on his outside than the actual event that brought about his end.

It's how men like Alex work, though.

It's how men like me do not.

FATHER KNOWS BEST? MY DAD KNEW JACK

"Suddenly in his home," my father says, scoffing—but he always sounded like this whenever he read the obits. "Why do they print it like that? Do they really think we don't know?" He'd been this way for longer than I could remember. He knew the reason, too, the why of it, but just didn't care. Now that I think about it, it pretty much summed up the man I came from better than I ever could have.

It didn't frighten or disgust me, but it did make me feel for him—that a person I loved was as emotionally stunted as he. Kitchen chair scrapping against linoleum, he continues: "And what's your two cents there, Cubby? You have a stance?"

I don't want to answer, don't want to chance a fight. Not that I was being left much of a choice, mind you. Also: Cubby? He hadn't called me that in years. Right here, this should have sent my spider-sense reeling.

"I think you know my answer, Dad."

He chuckled. "Agree to disagree, is that it?"

"Whatever you need it to be, Dad. You expecting Mom soon?" He did, and so did I, which was the entire reason for my presence.

"She called—said she'd be no later than five." I look at my watch, sigh as I do the math. Last time we'd been alone in the same room for an extended period had been when Allie died—when my father failed to resuscitate his first-born child. My sister's death left a void in our lives and in our relationship, as well. Each of us, from that day on, requiring a much bigger boat.

It had been a chicken bone, nothing more, but Herman Shanks never believed his son could do what he himself was certain he was supposed to do. This is my take on it, anyway. I'm sure if you were to ask him, you would get something else entirely. That day revised, perhaps.

"How're things with the store?"

The store was Walmart, but the position I held sucked, and don't let anybody ever tell you management is otherwise. "Store's good, Dad." I lied. "Christmas rush up and in swing." And then I smiled, feeling far from myself by doing so. My Dad, though, he lets it slide—his one true kindness. Always said he couldn't stand awkwardness and the elbows it creates.

"'Bout that time, is it?"

I couldn't tell whether it was a question. I ask for a beer instead. Then I re-check my watch. Damn thing was going backward—must be, I thought. Surprising me, my father says this: "I'm the reason you're here, Matt." We are sitting in the La-Z-Boys now, me in mom's, he in his, when he interjects this into the small talk we'd become.

I look at him, at the rough lines of his face. When his eyes do not lift to meet mine, I know for sure I have entered—*Danger, Will Robinson, danger*—a territory I had yet to tread: my father's entire demeanor at this moment contrasted with everything I had ever known. Did I know what was coming next, this remark but a prelude to his master plan? I can say I did not. Everything said and done, it didn't change the way I felt about him, either; the boat he had placed me on had long since sailed.

"I wanted to apologize. For everything. You know what I'm talking about?"

"I think I might." I take a sip of beer, wondering how I had stumbled into an episode of *The Twilight Zone.* At any second Rod Serling would come out and say: *You are about to meet a man, a man who always had to be right, who only lived to control the people he loved.* Why do these types of images invade my thoughts? I don't know. If I were a shrink, though (let alone a betting man), I'm pretty sure my money would be on my room, my movies and TV, and how my father's retreat had forced me there.

"I was wrong is what I mean to say. About a lot of things. Especially your sister."

I am speechless. Apologizing, okay, but admitting he was wrong? This was not the man who raised me, not He Who Ruled With An Iron Fist. Where's the pod, I remember thinking.

"You know that church up on Brock?"

I did, somehow finding my voice and telling him so.

"If I'm to pinpoint it, I believe it started there. I'd been driving, Matt, that's all. They have this billboard out front where they put out little lines of scripture and such, changing it each week. I don't know if it was be- cause of the date—that it was around the time of Allie's death—or if it had been building up inside me and I was just unaware. Anyway, the little line up there that day was GOD ANSWERS KNEE-MAIL. All of a sudden I'm laughing, bustin' my gut, and then I'm crying, Matt, just as quick. Crying so hard that I have to pull over. You know my stance on God, on religion in general. It didn't make sense, Matt, none of it—know what I mean?"

I did, but not really. Except for weddings, his beliefs never allowed me to.

"You're telling me you found God?" That one released the Kraken, the one that Herman Shanks reserved for mouths too smart for their own good. It was only for a second, but still, it was there.

"Not God, no, but answers to questions I never knew I'd been asking."

"Dad," I say, suddenly annoyed. Had he really wrapped me up this easily? Was my yearning for an emotional connection with him so much larger than the hate I'd learned to control? Alas, I believe this might be the case. Pity the fool, I think, and wonder briefly what my wife would say if I came home with a mohawk like Clubber Lang's.

"You," my father blurts, his eyes suddenly on mine. "It's you I did wrong. You, who need answers as to why I'm this way. And I wish I could give them to you, Matt, I really do, but I don't know how. All I can say is that I am aware I did you wrong; that it was always me, never you." And then he cries. Six-two, two-forty, arms like iron from years of construction, reduced to a puddle of heaving, horse-like sobs. I want to run. I want to scream. I get up instead, on my way to console the man who let my sister die the day I turned fifteen. Honestly, I could be a poster child.

I want to ask why—why he wouldn't let me do what I'd been trained to do. Why he had pushed me aside as he tried to extract the bone with fingers that could not reach. Mostly, though, mostly it was the blade I envisioned, and how for the love of God he thought he could perform a procedure he'd only seen on TV.

Done, we hug again, and then we talk a little more. I never ask him those questions though—the ones I'd been lugging around for years. Did it make it right? That I now wished to remain as detached as he'd been since Allie's death? Not really, no, but it's really all I'd ever known. And this problem I have—this addiction to all things pop culture? We'll include it. Sure. How could I not? I will give my father credit, though, as he was not built like other men. Emotionally, I mean. His smile, however—there at the door as he helps me into my coat—this is what I will remember most: how genuine it looked, how free.

Shortly I would come to understand why.

His funeral was on a Wednesday, my mother being the one who found him in what used to be my room. It was also she who asked me to write his obituary for the paper. I said okay, beginning with: *Suddenly in his home...*

Deep down, I feel he would approve.

PAPER OR PLASTIC

"The little guy at the end of the bar?" They're not as quiet as they believe, the big one being the loudest.

"Him, yup." The smaller one thrusts out his jaw as he says this. Unlike his partner, he sports a ball cap, the Reds, and a piece of fur trying its best to resemble a beard. "Fucker's more than hardcore. Mental more like." He wasn't far off, not as far as my social worker was concerned. Eight months on and still she insists I call every day. Court ordered or not, sticks in my craw like Orville Redenbacher himself went in there and made the deposit. "Took all his co-workers at once and made applesauce is what I heard. Drugged them to sleep and then piled 'em in a baler. You know how much pressure one a them machines holds?"

The big guy says no and laments his desire for another beer. I take a pull from my own and think back to that day—to how each of their faces looked as I offered them juice. Florence had been the only one to rebuff me that day, but after a while even she came around. Makes me realize I always enjoyed the floral department most of all. I truly did.

"Something like eighteen thousand pounds per square inch. You fuckin' imagine?" A truer number would be three thousand or so. Still got the job done, no matter how one tried to slice it.

"No, Dave. I can't imagine. What I can is you buying my ass the beer you owe me." Ah, trouble in paradise. My favorite kind.

I get up, limp closer, and plop myself two barstools from where they look on. "Would you fellas like to know what I learned from such an experience?" They stare at me, one second, two, and then the little guy, Dave, he laughs like I just told the world's best joke.

I took it as a yes.

While not tall, the bigger guy's name is Lance, and it's to him I look as I begin. His grey hair is receding and slicked back, running counter to the stuff erupting from his forearms and chest. It gave him a Popeye-like quality, but a Popeye who ate more burgers than green veg. "I learned you get fucked in the ass either way." I was not speaking figuratively. The opposite, in fact. My cellmate letting me know in no uncertain terms that a measuring contest was not to come, not in the ways I might think. Might have been okay if I'd been given a turn or two, but no, it fails to happen in the six years we are cellies. "And do you know what this big bad man does just before he makes release? He sells me, my mouth and ass quite the commodity, I'm told."

Look, I get it. Most of us want to be understood,

right? Sure. Fine. Now I look back, it even becomes one of the core reasons I went and did what I did. Sure, lots of my co-workers treated me as they shouldn't have, Mr. Gray especially, but if there's one thing I take pride in during my time on the inside, it's this: I have come to agree with the state and take ownership for my part in what went down.

I have to become better at being better, is all. I have to try and fit back in.

I mean, wasn't anybody else who pushed the button on the side of that machine, right?

"So what, you're some kinda queer now? Move it back down to the end of the bar if that's the case, fuck-o." You think people can't amaze you more than they already do. Bravo, Dude. You're a man who sticks his landings.

"Nope," I say, and motion to the bartender for three more beers. "Still like girls. The forced sausage aspect is just me letting you know that nothing changes, not really. Not in. Not out. It's all the same. The only thing to hold on to is what we believe in from the start." It works. I win them over. And by the time we close the bar they are three sheets to the wind, and I am not. I am something else.

I am Rage.

"Remember: you don't have to immerse yourself, Ronald, but you should be putting a little bit of yourself out there every day." Leslie Muldoon. The social worker assigned to my case, during one of the many calls to discuss my tendencies and how they worried her so. She's tall, black, and has quite an attractive smile. What she doesn't have is clue one as to how a person like me is to put themselves "out there." "Maybe join a book club. Do you like to read? Maybe a gamer club. I'd like to see you do something, Ronald. You've earned it. No matter what anyone says, you have paid your debt to society."

She was right, of course. Twelve years hard time until someone decides to reopen my case and then it's suddenly four more in a psych ward of someone else's choosing. That's not the funny part. What *is* becomes what Leslie has repeated *ad nauseam* these last eight months.

You have paid your debt to society.

Unfortunately, society has yet to pay mine.

My new friends and I walk on, my story of balers and body parts spurring them on. I am a hero to them. Someone who has stuck it to the man. I have heard it said before, and I will hear it said again: you can't fix stupid.

We make our way to Metro Foods, my hand curled tightly to my chest. Inside, there's only one cashier that I can see. She's chewing gum and reading a *Us Weekly*. Oh, the days.

I walk the entire store, counting off the rest of the night crew as I do. Three in total. All in the cereal aisle putting up stock. One bubble-fronted fat man surrounded by two pimple-faced Asians listening to iPods. I think it will work. I believe it can.

Back to Dave and Lance, I find them in the confectionary section, Lance deep into a Three Musketeers. I give them a nod to the left and, once beckoned, they come. *Employees Only* marks the double doors we go through, and we don't even have to look for the baler, it being just off to the right. It's smaller than the one we had at Mister Food, but no less rectangular. For them to fit I would have to bend them somewhat, but that wasn't going to be the hard part.

Listening to them was.

"And you're telling me you fit thirty people into *that?*" Of course this was the first question, size being everything and all.

"No. The one I used was bigger."

"That's what *she* said!" And then Dave, oh master of one-upmanship, in light of the story I was trying to tell about my time on the inside, guffaws: "No-no-no, that's what *he* said!"

I sigh. I can't help myself. To the left of us stand skids of stock not yet processed, lined against the wall. On either side of the baler sit shopping carts, some with product in them, some without. They notice I'm not laughing when they see the tin of peaches in my hand. Only Lance tilts his head slightly before he drops from the impact. Dave turns to run but stumbles, the back of his head receiving what the front of Lance's just had. If I'm anything more than what I was before I went in, it's this: stronger. The years away granted me the time to build myself up physically. It helps as I load them up and over the baler's top lip—up on my shoulder and then down within. I see there is cardboard inside this baler, halfway from the top. It brings back memories of Mr. Gray and how he instructed me to never mix cardboard and plastic when producing a bale. He'd said this in front of them all, saying it as if I were someone new.

I press the button, there on the side of this machine.

Green, it performs as programmed, screeching to life and cycling its way down. I press it again. Again. Hold it until I begin to scream. Unable to stop, my throat becomes fire, my neck like cord. I hear bones collapse. I watch blood escape.

Before I'm hit from behind, I have time to think: people will understand this time.

Perhaps they'll even try.

FAMILY MEETING

I repeat that I love her—that I always have. Not because she needs to be reminded but because she must remember with whom she is dealing. She does this, she becomes open to the changes I'm suggesting. I'm not just talking about the psychologists and the psychiatrists, or even the medications we both had a hard time sounding out, either. I'm talking about overkill, the life, and all the ninja bullshit—shit I'll admit I should have put a stop to long ago.

"Like you, I want a different outcome. To go at things head-on instead of sideways like we did." I loosen my grip on her neck, enough so she can breathe easier than she had been. We stand at the island counter as one, my words coming to her from behind. All told, not even close to how I envisioned this playing out. It wasn't going to be easy, agreed, but this? This had become something else entirely. "Granted, you are a bit more attached, and I give you this, but I believe it's only because it was you who carried him."

In hindsight, perhaps I shouldn't have given Ricky as

much responsibly as I did. For the record, I did have reservations before I sent him to collect from Chen. It wasn't as overt as last time, not really, but it still got me thinking in ways no father should. "But to take Chen's son as he did, how can one foresee and defend against something like that?" I reach around, restart the video on my phone, and the process of watching a man lose his head begins anew.

Two sons come into focus, ours and Chen's, one in a chair, the other not. We watch Ricky zip up his suit, lower his goggles, and as he brings the chainsaw to life we hear him proclaim *this is what happens when you fail to comply*. It causes Chen's son to struggle in a whole new way. Ricky was good, though—the amount of duct tape from chest to abdomen enough to still any movement, frantic or otherwise. Up and through, it happens in less time than it takes Ricky to bring the machine back down to his side. Not yet finished, my son makes one more pass, but delicately, slicing up the left arm like some kind of goddamn surgeon.

He goes in, grabs the top bone, the radius, the ulna, what-fucking-ever, and by the third pull it comes free, the muscle and skin still attached coming with it in strips. He looks to the camera, uses the bone as a pointing stick, and says: "Any questions?"

I turn off my phone, lay it face down beside a half-eaten plate of pie.

"You see? Something like this cannot be defended against, Sharon. Plain and simple." I'm right in her ear now, my voice low and to the point. She stands still, breathes, but her heart remains a hammer. "One *is* able to react, though. And I know what you're thinking, I do,

110

but you knew exactly what you were getting into the day you put on that ring. I had enemies then. I have enemies now. Everything we've done, everything we do, it all has consequences." Would she come round? The possibility existed. The pill was a tough one, though—more jagged than anything most would ever have to swallow.

"You might be too young to even remember this, but there's this movie, Old Yeller, and we have more in common with it than I care to admit." Our boy was quite a bit more than a rabid dog, sure, but the point she needed to concentrate on was the very same point she was refusing to understand: no matter how I spun things, how inconceivable it all seemed, what I did, it had to be done. Chen, he wouldn't have let go.

"That being said, *I'm* going to let go. Once I have, I want the knife to stay where it is. That happens, we can begin to move on. We do that, we can even discuss how fortunate it was I married a much younger woman and how it was your age that helped tip the scales." I step back, doing so until my backside hits the fridge. I await either fury or concession, belief or disdain. I receive none of the above, and deep down I have to admit I expected as much. Only when she turns and her shoulders dip do I realize her journey to my side of the table has begun. I say this not to gloat or to cut into any part of her grief. I say it because self-preservation and a realist are the same damn thing.

"Who knows, this time we may even have a girl."

ADVICE, FREE OR OTHERWISE

If there's anything you need to know about me it's this: I
have always been open to trying new things. All told, it's
the reason it's me standing here and not Clive or Mitchy
D. Coulda been either one in a heartbeat, sure, and
maybe things woulda turned out better for you in the
long run had this been the case, Sal. I can certainly picture something like that. Sure. No problem. I've never
been particularly good at declining these types of situations, though. Better suited at going along than getting
along if the truth is what we're attempting here.

You'd think this wouldn't be the case, with me jawin'
up a storm like I am, but things have a way of turning
opposite to what you want sometimes. Know what I
mean? S'okay. I know you know it's coming. Can tell
you see it in my one good eye. Good thing or bad, it's
inevitable is what this is—something the both of us will
come to agree upon.

What I won't do, Sal, is take the blame. I'll take some,
sure, as I am a man who enjoys his work immensely, but I

will not take it all. If you woulda just paid what you owed when you owed it nothing like what I represent is put into motion. But no. Not you. You choose an alternate route, and boom, here we are, the two of us in the back of your kitchen, these big bad ovens selling their wares.

Oh, come on now, it's not like you didn't know something like this could occur. You own a pizza joint for crying out loud. It would be damn well remiss of me if I didn't use the tools you use on a daily basis to send the message I have been paid to deliver. Above all else, I am professional to my core.

A person like you doesn't want to believe such a thing, and I can't blame you for that, not fully, not with you sittin' here listening to me as you are. Then again, it's you who are in the wrong here, Sal, with no one to fault but your pretty blue self. One hundred and ten grand might not be as huge as it once was, no, but once you factor in the juice and extra week Big Ron already gave you it turns into something men like me can only dream of.

Means I was called the morning of, Sal.

Means I went and got your wife and daughter before I went and got you.

Means I prepped them before you woke up and each should be ready just about the time I pop open these doors.

I like these pizza retrievers, too. Very authentic, Sal. Let's you get right in there, all the way to the back. And looky here, just look how the cheese and the sides of their faces have blended themselves together. Seamlessness is what we are witnessing here, Sal. It took more than a steady hand, too, but you know what wouldn't leave my thoughts, once the peeling process began? Sticky Tack. You old enough to remember Sticky Tack, Sal? Of course you are. You know what else you're old enough for?

Advice, Sal. Free or otherwise.

It means it can get worse than this. If you don't take to heart what I'm saying to you now. Means your parents could come into the equation, or your brother and his wife for that matter. Maybe those triplets they had the misfortune of having as well. That happens, a trip may or may not have to be taken to that other restaurant you own, the one where I'm told the steak ain't half bad.

You understand the picture I'm painting for you here?

If anything, it makes you out to be smaller than I know you to be. A pretty harsh assessment, sure, but still a thing that needs to be considered, especially when coupled with the type of man I feel you believe you are.

It's how you keep people like me out of your kitchen, Sal.

More importantly, it stops us from attempting new things.

LIKE-MINDED INDIVIDUALS
A Bishop Rider Story

When I mention life has always been about choice, I'm not telling you anything new. I think you're going to want to be comfortable, is all. Shoe on the other foot and all, I know I'd want to be. Mind if I open a window, though? This trailer of yours, no offense, but it could really use some air.

There—better. Now listen, Pete, me and you, we're gonna go over some stuff here. Things you probably know and stuff you're gonna wish your mind could erase. It's all you though, bud. Every bit. You may think otherwise, sure, and hey, that's your right. But I should enlighten you to the type of man I am. I'm the type who believes in doing his homework, Pete. A man who believes it is better to know than it is to assume. With what's comin', you'd be wise to remember as much.

So, the elephant in the room. Bishop Rider. Ring any bells? Mm-huh. I thought it might. Let's you and I go one better, though. You see this nail gun? For the moment, let's pretend it's Rider. Now put out your hand.

117

Flatter.

No, *flatter.*

Good. Now picture your hand being all the things wrong with this world. You doing that, Pete? No, come on, lemme see your eyes. Good. Now, I pull this trigger, it unleashes something that has already occurred: a man who has had enough. A man who will not put up with one bit more.

Ready, then?

Cool. And would you look at that—now we have ourselves a base! Looks like it smarts some, too. It could hurt more, though. Oh, yes. Loads. It could hurt as much as, say, losing a mother and a sister might hurt.

You see where it is I might be going with this, Pete?

Sure you do. I know you do. A refresher of sorts might be in order it seems. Something to get the juices flowing, no?

Abrum gave the order, this we know. But of the brothers, which Abrum had it actually been? Marty or Marcel? I don't think it much mattered, not once we got to the guts of things. At the beginning, though, when I first met Rider, when he ventilated the back of Marty Abrum's head into his fettuccini alfredo, this was an entirely different story—the man all heat and grief and rage, lashing out at the world the only way he knew how. Me, this is where I come in, me being an associate of *your* brother and all.

Before we get to that, however, I must mention Batista. John Batista, he's Rider's guy on the inside. They used to be partners, back before Bishop threw in the badge. This is how we stay one step ahead of guys like you, Pete. How we've chosen to take the lot of you down.

The look on your face leads me to believe you disagree with this. If I'm wrong, please, forgive me, but as a rebuttal, let me then ask you this: was it your brother who decided to force Rider's family into the van that day, or was it you? Yes, Pete. We know. The surveillance video they found—it's the very reason we sit across from each other now. Better yet, it's the very reason we haven't allowed your dogs to eat this entire last week.

What? You think a beatdown and a nail gun was gonna be the worst of it?

Pete. Pete, m'man.

Six men in masks fucked April Rider to her death, the Abrum brothers filming and distributing the entirety for all the world to see. This over and above the murder of Maggie Rider, who'd been guilty of one thing and one thing only: showing up in the wrong place at the wrong time. I mean, Pete, truly, if it'd been you, can you say you would have responded differently?

But it wasn't you: I can tell that's what you're thinking. Among other things, of course. But it was you, Pete. Only not as you think. It's why we need to talk about Richie now. We've tried, but we seem unable to locate that brother of yours. He'll turn up eventually, sure, but we want to do this our way, on our terms. Oh, did I say we?

Yup. Sure did. Didn't even hear him come up behind you, did you? Nimble as fuck for such a big guy, ain't he? Brings us to the main event if I'm to be completely honest. I'll make you a deal, though. A last-ditch effort to save yourself some pain. You tell us where Richie's been holing himself up and we'll let you keep the hand a few minutes more. Fair enough, yes? Though retain is a far better word in a situation such as this, I think. The alternative being something not many people know and something that is going to happen regardless of the scenario you choose. Dogs, once starved, they tend to eat slower than one might think. Either way, it comes back to what I mentioned earlier: comfort. Not only how we view it, Pete, but how we choose to embrace it.

How it can be twisted to meet a certain level of need.

Fast or slow, both hands or not, it allows me to promise you this: your dogs, Pete, they're about to eat like kings.

HEAVIER THAN IT OUGHT TO BE

I've blocked memories. I know that now. By disclosing this, I would have to say I've blocked certain types of feelings as well. I mean, it's the only thing that makes sense, really, and goes a long way in supporting the reasons why I never connected with my mother. Speaking of Rebecca Chalmers, you know *how* I've come to know this? First reason, top of the list, would be her. That she's a right fuck of a cunt. Second in line would be the old home movies I found up under the stairs in the house I grew up in. These were movies I was not meant to see. That I was the star of said movies, well, that's the reason I'm doing this, I suppose. Stuff like this, the stuff I found, it does something deep within you, toward your core, where the filling of who you are either breaks or continues on.

There are only those two choices in situations like this. To this I can fucking attest.

I am suggesting that one day your life seems good, or what you've come to accept as good, and the next it's falling apart, smashed beyond repair. After that it becomes something more, festering, and you either live long enough to decide it's time to eat iron or you simply carry on. Decided, a drive is formed, consuming you, and suddenly it's revenge that lights the way. Except it isn't suddenly, not at all, as it has always been there, a desire you could never fully explain or have reason to act upon. It's thick, this feeling, and red, the blood in your veins somehow heavier than it ought to be. You have any idea what I'm talking about? Then perhaps I should go on.

I have a sister. Her name is Paula. She's okay. Sometimes a bitch, yes, but mostly she's okay. She is short and squat, carrying a little extra weight in the places women would rather not. Paula is pretty enough, though, in ways I can appreciate even though she's my sib. Same as me, Paula has no use for the woman we came from, never has, and so when Ma gets sick, well, let's just say there was some drawing of straws and such. I lost, you see, and this is where it begins to fall apart. To *really* fall apart. My life, I mean. Clarity, Ben, clarity. That is what I'm looking for. What I am trying to convey. Please stand by.

"You should move in with her. Really, you should." This is my sister's idea of humor. It's not that I don't appreciate it. Far from it, matter of fact. It's that I'm unable to use such digs that has gotten my goat. I flip Paula off instead. Weak, yes, and I wish I had more, but short straw, you see.

"I'll make you a deal then," she says. I take my eyes from the *Seinfeld* rerun, the one with Uncle Leo and the watch. Paula makes me wait, though, there on the couch—takes the last big pull on her beer before slamming the bottle down harder than she needs to. "I'll split you the cost to put her in, or up, or whatever you fucking call committing her. I sure as hell don't want to be wiping her ass when my turn comes around is what I'm saying. What say you to that, Bub?" It was never Ben with Paula—just Bub. Always Bub.

I look at her, at my older sister who looked more like our father than I, and then get each of us another Bud. It's here I should probably say I don't hate women, not totally, though an argument could be made regarding such a statement. I say it nonetheless. As I don't hate women, not all of them, and I didn't hate my mother up until a month ago, when I unearthed this depravity that has somehow escaped my memory. How I suppressed such a thing I will never know, but now that I've *seen*, whoa-fucka, is someone gonna pay. I mean, all things being equal, she pretty much has to.

So I say to Paula, "Sure, why not, it's not like *I* really wanted to wipe her ass, either." And then we laugh, my sister and I, there on a Tuesday, nine days before I decide that I *will* be wiping my mother's ass. Along with a few other things, I might add. I will do this because of what I found, these movies under the stairs, and I will do it because I have chosen to take Rebecca Chalmers on, illness and all, even though Paula and I agreed to commit her. Paula didn't seem to care when I changed my mind, either, just told me I was a fuck-head, and that it was nobody's funeral but my own. If Paula had known, though, if I had told her what I had found and watched as I was boxing up our mother's stuff...

I wondered if she would help.

And then I wondered if Paula knew.

I would have to be sure and ask Ma—that's what I've decided—what I'd ask her every day as I beat her with a stick in the basement of her house. I would also ask her what she believes a monster is made of; if his stuff was as stern as it looked. Bad enough my contemptible father did what he did, yes, and that the piece-of-shit taped it, but what upsets me more is that she—she was *there*. How do I know this for certain? I've thought about that. Thought about it often, matter of fact. I could live with it, I suppose, if it'd only been him, and only because he is dead and gone and I never have to see him again. But in the last box I went through, near the bottom of the pile, I found a tape among the Super 8s. It was VHS, this tape. Recordable. And as I watched...movement. Not just my father plugging away at every orifice I owned, but actual fucking movement from the actual fucking camera that was recording the actual fucking images of my innocence being quashed. You see what I'm saying? You see what I mean? I mean, seriously, it's as though she was panning around in search of the best possible angle there was to get it all from. It led to the first question in a long line of what will prove not only Rebecca Chalmers' undoing, but that of mine as well: Just who the fuck was holding the camera then?

Who, Ma? *Who?*

RESTY ACRES

In the beginning I didn't believe him, nor would you, all told. The tip-off should have been the coffee he brought me.

In the six years I had known Emil Dimpton he'd never given up anything to anyone free of charge. In his infinite wisdom (add sarcasm here) I think he thought buying me my morning Joe should have made me more inclined to believe his tale of fancy. He'd been wrong, of course, as I have already stated, but only for a while. In the end—and perhaps even more so in the middle—I came to believe as much as he. God, I say, should help us all.

My name is Walter Meade and I am seventy-six years old. I'm writing this because there needs to be an account of what went on here—what *is* going on here. Just as I did not believe Emil there at the beginning, no one has believed it coming from my mouth, either. Of this I am sure, and the reason I have chosen to detail it this way instead. I will write and make copies and send them by mail. It will appear as though I am sick, the conclusions drawn unavoidable—that I am a senile old fart, sane but for a lurking dementia. This is the risk I take. This is how scared I am. With what life I have left, I wish to remain.

As you are aware, I am crippled, my wife and legs lost to me long ago, both to the same event. I live in this retirement home that someone—some young upstart, I've no doubt—decided to call Resty Acres. Funny, huh? That name? Resty Acres. No, not really. Kind of sad, actually, when you think about it. It is a nice enough place, very quiet, very clean, consisting of a menu that still finds ways to surprise me. Also, I have yet to be beaten since my eldest dropped me here some eight years ago. And just so we're clear, I don't hold it against you, Barry, for leaving me here like you did. You are the oldest, the responsibility fell to you. If it were me in your shoes, I would have done the same. Not only because I had become a burden, but because you have your own family to take care of now. I am old now, yes, what more could someone like me have to offer someone like you? Even though I brought you into this world, fed you and clothed you, nurtured and guided you, ensured you received your schooling and then your doctoring, I don't deserve anything in return. Nothing. As you've given, son—as you've given. I wish you well, boy. As I do your brothers and sisters.

Pricks. The lot of you. Am I Bitter? Little bit.

Back to it then.

It was a Tuesday when Emil came to me with the free cup of Joe. And right from the get-go you could tell something was off, that the man was struggling, as if some unseen weight was pulling at his corners, the ones that keep the majority of us in check. For an old codger awaiting his last day, he was an unusually upbeat fellow, but he was far from upbeat on this particular day. No, on this particular day Emil was scared. I would go so far as to say terrified even. His color was off, as well, his face almost ashen except for the dark circles that hung beneath his eyes like used tea bags—the round kind, not the square. He kept wiping his head, too, with that damn handkerchief of his, which would have been much weirder if the old boy had still had hair. Slowly, he explained as best he could what had happened. When he was finished, he pleaded with me to believe him, adding that he didn't think anyone else would. I agreed with him, as what he told me sounded like poppycock, but balderdash was the word I think I used.

"But Walter, it took Vera! I don't want to be next."

"And you won't be," I said, my voice not quite as sympathetic as maybe it should have been. "Emil, if what you say is true, then size will prove your friend. It makes you too big for it to take you. Besides, how do you know Vera hasn't had one of her episodes and simply went wandering, as she's been known to do? You don't. Therefore, until she turns up, you cannot know. Not for sure."

He looked at me then, and I could tell his confusion remained, thicker now than when he first sat down. This had not been my intent.

Around and around his handkerchief went, damn thing wiping whatever it needed to wipe. He said: "But I am losing weight every week, Walter. I weigh only a little more than one hundred and twenty as of this morning. I am very close to the pattern weight, I think."

"Emil, seriously, we are too old to believe in things such as these. There are no vampires, especially ones who eat their victims. When have you ever heard of a vampire doing that? How would it be possible even? Don't they go only for the jugular, the drinking of blood and what-not?"

"Do not patronize me, Walter!" And there was real anger there, a flash of it anyway. "Three of us have gone missing in the last two years, four now with Vera. All unaccounted for. Off wandering they say, always in the middle of the night, all of it conveniently blamed on se-nility, of course. Do you think I have not thought this through? Do you not think I have seen?"

"Emil, you yourself said it was dark and you couldn't really see."

"But the noises I heard!"

"Yes. But hadn't those awakened you?" But it was too late. He was up and gone without so much as a backward glance, that damn handkerchief searching for something, searching as always. It was only later that I realized I hadn't even popped the lid to the coffee Emil had gotten me. I'm sure if some shrink thought hard enough, they would be able to form some sort of correla-tion between this and what was about to happen.

Yes, quite sure.

I didn't see Emil much after that morning, and when I did, he didn't look any better than he had when he first told me about the vampire who was hidden amongst the elderly here at Resty Acres. His appearance was declin-ing, deteriorating little by little each time I saw him in the weeks that followed. I don't know exactly when it happened, but there came a time when he chose to no longer dress himself. Moreover, his hygiene was beginning to suffer. Ultimately, he ended up wearing nothing more than underpants and that housecoat of his, the one with black stripes. He still had his handkerchief, though, that same old red one, although it seemed to be getting less and less work each time I saw him; mostly I would see it dangling from his hand, limp as his new demeanor. It was when Emil himself went missing that things began to change for me. Or rearrange, if I'm honest, when the talk Emil and I had had on that Tuesday morning was given new perspective.

I am very close to the pattern weight, I think.

That is what he had said, there at our table in the breakfast room. Odd, yes, but as I think back over the times I saw him wandering to and fro in that housecoat of his, it occurs to me that Emil's weight, indeed, seemed to be on the decline. The man was becoming smaller and thinner each time I saw him. Thinking back, maybe I could have prevented some of this—maybe, maybe not. At least I could have put forth an effort. I am ashamed that I did not, just so you know, as it places my character in a new light, one I am unfamiliar with.

Before all that, however, I received a new roommate. His name was Stanley Chesterfield, and if that name isn't a handle then I don't know what is. I called him Flat Stan on account of his face, which really needs no further explanation. He was a smaller man, and frail, from years of bed rest, I'm sure. He was also uncommunicative. Not totally, but unable to hold a conversation about the here and now. Poor Flat Stan had come to be my roomy while he found himself trapped within the end stages of Alzheimer's. This prison, Alzheimer's, is a disease no one would wish upon their worst enemy. It is rampant here at Resty Acres, perhaps the disease de jour, and believe you me when I say it is as powerful as it is heart-wrenching. A fear of mine I'll admit, but no longer my number one. No, that place is now reserved for the impossible proved possible, for the stuff I used to know as make-believe.

I have looked evil in the eye, my friend. I am afraid to say it does not blink.

A meeting was called concerning Emil's disappearance, the entire residence escorted into the auditorium before lunch three days after the search had been called off. The smell was there, of course, as it always is. And don't think we are immune, because we aren't. We know it's there, hanging over and rising from us like an invisible prophet. The death smell is what I'm referring to, the yellow smell of the elderly, of chemical and approaching death. In a room such as ours, with more than two hundred seniors...well...you get the drift—no pun intended.

Dr. Hamilton is the guy who runs the show here, the Big Tuna as it were, and he has done so since before my children decided to make me a member. He's a slick one, is Dr. Hamilton, he and that new-age ponytail of his. I didn't know how slick he was until after this meeting. Oh, yes. Indeed. It was when he started in on how Emil had been battling what I had previously called the disease de jour that I really began to see the situation for what it was: a railroad, as in we were being taken for a ride.

Emil Dimpton never had any such disease. This I know.

We were then informed that stronger security measures would be in place by week's end. This action would be taken in light of the "now recurring" and "very unfortunate" theme that had found its way into the "very heart" of Resty Acres itself—that with Emil's disappearance as well as Vera's (lest we forget Hickman and Robalard, whom he did not mention by name, just so we are clear) the board had gathered (in the eleventh hour, I'm sure) and voted unanimously in favor of a new mandate, one that was to be "swift and immediate" in its "execution and implementation." Ah. How nice. They care! They really, really care.

"Dr. Hamilton?" I asked.

"Walter, yes, you have a question?" Not Mr. Meade. Walter. There you go.

"Yes," I said and paused, momentarily wishing for the deadwood to work once more. I wanted to stand as I said my piece, is all. No reason why, just did—just something that happens to me from time to time. For the most part, I'm good with what my situation is, having come to terms with it moons ago, but still, as I've said, it happens. "I have known Emil for six years," I continued. "In that time, I have never seen any of the symptoms you associate with Alzheimer's. How can he have just wandered off? What I'm asking is, are you sure?"

I half expected to see something register in Hamilton's eyes, a darting flash of guilt perhaps, some glaring sheen of hatred. What I received instead was something quite the opposite. Squatting to his knees, the man offered me a tenderness I was up until that point unaware he possessed. He said, "Walter. Emil was someone you probably saw on a regular basis, was he not? Your friend, maybe?

This never makes us the best judges, on our best days. I am a trained physician and Alzheimer's is my specialty: I would know. Emil was suffering. Silently. And it was coming on fast toward the end, before he went missing. It comes as no surprise that many of you failed to notice." And the slick bastard had me, honestly; hook, line, and ponytail. It was when he threw in the wink, there at the end, that two things became very clear, very fast. One was that it had always been an inside job, just as Emil had suspected from the get-go. Two was that I had just made myself a target.

Now...it is not like any overt changes occurred once Dr. Hamilton let me in on the little secret Emil had been silenced for. No long looks from across the room when I saw him in one of the lounges or many of the hallways or anything like that. Neither was there hissing or the producing of fangs, just so you know. Everything remained as it had been before the latest disappearances, Resty Acres reverting back to what it had always been— a retirement home, the kind that serves Jell-O after each and every meal.

I was neither hounded nor touched. Even though I now knew, and Dr. Hamilton knew I knew, I remained alive. And don't get me wrong, I do not know for certain that Dr. Hamilton is the vampire Emil spoke of, only that he is part of the conspiracy residing here.

Days passed, weeks. And as most of you know, I tried to get the word out, calling as many of you as I could. Do you remember that, Barry? Do your brothers and sisters? How do you recall the times I called and tried to convince you of the plight I faced? What did they tell you when you called back to inquire about the state of your father's mental health? What I think they told you is what I believe they tell all who inquire about the darkness that goes on here; do they apologize and tell you it's senility setting in? Perhaps a bit of the early Alzheimer's even? *We'll do some tests though, yes, yes, a batch of them, and get back to you with the results.* Did it go a little something like that, Barry? I'm pretty sure it did.

Do you see how slick this makes them?

Do you?

Human beings are complex individuals. We are also simple, and at times, stupidly so. Like many of us, not much scares me anymore. Some things, yes, like disease and war, but none of it gutting me as completely as it had when I was a boy.

I am a talker and always have been, loud with opinions. It tends to lead people to believe I am cantankerous by nature, and an ass-hole by choice. I am not, however, but far too old and much too tired to explain it away in the document before you. If my wife were alive she would verify the things I have just mentioned. My kids? Not so much. And that is their choice. It was always my way or the highway beneath the roof I built above their heads. I was a stern parent—the need for them to know and understand respect was at the very top of our list. This is all I will say about that. They know their bed and how they must lie in it. What I must get back to is the fear I mentioned earlier, the stuff from my childhood. It is back inside me now, a thing come home to roost. Unwilling to relent, it screams for release.

I have seen the creature at work is what I mean to say. As Emil Dimpton believed, it does do more than drink.

I had gotten used to Flat Stan's snoring. Not that I had much choice in the matter, with him sleeping most of the time. When he did awaken we would talk about the old days, when the grass was greener and all that jazz. During these conversations I was usually somebody else, a Johnny or a Duncan, sometimes a David. This didn't bother me, and poor Flat Stan never knew the difference. I think he did come close to the surface once, as there was a pause and then the question of how I ended up in the wheelchair. When I began to tell him my story he asked me what I was talking about and whether I thought mother would approve. At this I was back to being Duncan, the older of his two sons. This was how my relationship played with Flat Stan—two parts sleep, one part conversational window into his past. Realizing this forces me to acknowledge that Alzheimer's is not unlike the creature that stalks me, that both are draining forces of utter destruction, time and method the only differences I can find between them.

It was the very night I came to this realization that the vampire awakened me—overrode the snores to which I had adapted. Rising to consciousness, I came to know of the sucking sounds Emil had spoken of months ago, the ones that now replaced Flat Stan's exhalations. Poor Flat Stan—there would be no more stories concerning Johnny or Duncan, or sometimes a David. I am certain the man was dead before I turned on my reading lamp. In doing so I bear witness to the thing I am writing about, to that which has been preying upon us here at Resty Acres. I can't say for sure it's a vampire, not in the truest sense. What I can say is it shares a lot of the same characteristics that you and I have been shown in movies and on TV. Not all, but some. Other things reminded me of leeches, similar to the ones I used to fish with.

Big doesn't do it justice—the thing was massive, six-five, I'd guess, from head to boot. It was wide, as well. Bent over, its mouth and chin were buried in the middle of Stan's chest as it drank, its throat bulging until I thought it might burst. You would think my turning on the light and sitting up would make it notice me, yes? You would think I'd be screaming my fool head off for help, no? Both of these things should have happened but neither did. I watched as if hypnotized, stared as the vampire exsanguinated my roommate completely, listened as it sucked and swallowed and drank. Only when the draining was complete did it turn to me, then and not a moment before. I remained silent as it regarded me, lost within the caverns of its eyes. They were black like oil, those eyes, black like death, nothing of white at all. It moved toward me, touched me, a finger to my paunch. "Too much meat," it said, and the words were wet, still coated, swimming in the blood that used to run Stan. This is when my bladder let go, or when I believe it let go; I can't say for sure, couldn't then, can't now. After that it turned its attention back to Stan—to what remained of Stan. Standing over him it opened and closed its mouth, a *tocking* sound accompanying this. At the time I did not know it was flexing. Now, however, I do. It was readying itself, you see, ensuring the route was able.

Slowly at first, then faster, its mouth began to expand, widening to receive another set of fangs, ones that erupted first from the upper part of its jaw and then from the lower. As was the creature, so were the teeth: massive, long and sling-blade sharp.

You realize, of course, that the drinking was complete?

Okay. To the hole then, back into it being where it went. Slowly it leaned down and re-entered the open cavity in Stan's chest. I watched and listened as it latched on and created a seal between its mouth and Stan's wound. After this came another sound, this one louder than the first, the one it had been making with its jaw. It was deeper, too, coming from the breast bone it was making its way through. Once it did this, once it *broke* through—this is when I truly understood what Emil had been trying to convince me of that morning in the breakfast room, the day I patronized him more than a little bit.

I am very close to the pattern weight, I think.

I weigh only a little more than one hundred twenty as of this morning.

I think it can only consume around that much each time, roughly a hundred pounds a pull—its maximum, give or take. Amazing, no? A vampire who does it all! No fuss, no muss, no mess, no body. This is why it chooses the elderly, I think. Not only because we are probably the easiest of prey but because of the practicality we represent—that most of us are already the size it might require, each of us the lightest of light snacks.

The organs were next, all of them, and then the bones, followed, of course, by skin. All of it going, gone, as it continued to feed. Stan's body receded as it was depleted, everything being pulled up and into the supernatural vacuum it was attached to. The creature's throat became so engorged with the pressure it was creating that I thought its neck would burst open. And I don't know how, but I must have missed something, even though I witnessed it all. It never chewed, not once. I do not know whether it expelled some sort of compound while it was linked to Stan—whether this helped to liquefy what remained of him—because, as I've said, there was not an ounce of chewing, none. And last time I checked, human bones were still as hard as they ever were. It seems a logical assumption, right? That it might produce and secrete a toxin to help with what it devours? I know, I know: Where is the logic in *any* of this? I am most worried about what it said to me as it left, when it turned back from the door: *Soon,* it said; one word, nothing more. It was later that I noticed Stan's bed sheets—that even they did not remain. Whether taken or ingested I cannot say for sure.

That was four months ago. In the time between then and now, many things have occurred. The police were called, for one, and more than once, at that. After the third time I was dismissed with prejudice, informed I would be charged if another instance arose. I told this officer to shove it where the sun didn't shine and that if he felt so inclined then he should go ahead and do it, my pension would hold. Upon reflection I realize this was ill-advised at best. I was doing exactly what I was trying to avoid: no one will believe me, because the more I protest the more unstable I appear. Unstable leads to other words here at Resty Acres, words that begin with capital letters.

I have none of these impairments, however, and of that you can be sure—my faculties are intact, in tune without a touch. But this *is* protesting, is it not? Fine. I will say no more about it. Instead, I will tell you that I'm scared, that my fear remains.

Too much meat.

This is what it said to me, there in the room I shared with Stan. I know now it was referring to my weight, to the extra amount I had there. When you are suddenly paralyzed it is hard to maintain your previous body weight. Let no one tell you different. It seems you are only eating for half a body, and effectively you are, but the amount you had been used to, *that* doesn't go away—never has for me, anyway. What I'm trying to get across is that everything I ate seemed to fall and hold to the center of my body once my spine had been severed, the distribution lines breaking down somewhere along the way, the same line my spine had run upon, perhaps. Bottom line: I had a paunch, the creature touched it. At the time it did this I was roughly one-hundred-ninety pounds. It is not this I worry about, not anymore. That I have dipped below one hundred and twenty as of this morning is what concerns me—Emil-weight if you remember, on the day he brought me coffee. This is what terrifies me. Because I am unable to stop what is happening, having been stripped of a basic control. The creature did something to me, must have. Dr. Hamilton would disagree, I'm told, and has expressed as much. He thinks what I'm doing is to be commended, prolonging what he already sees as a long, full life. To his credit he kept a straight face. Have I told you how slick this man is? Yes, I think I have. He is not the vampire, though, as I think I have also mentioned. He is only a facilitator. Perhaps a disciple even, Resty Acres being the place he chooses to worship. I can only hope I will not die as the others have died, that I will remain uneaten. Tomorrow I will try again, after I have made copies and mailed them. I will need a key, however, and that is where you come in. Can you secure it? Moreover, will you? All the guards have one—it hangs from their shirts. They are new, these keys, no longer metal but instead made of plastic, each a rectangle in shape.

New security measures is what they said.

Too much meat.

Immediate and swift in implementation and execution; that is what they did.

I am very close to the pattern weight I think.

I can see now what they've done, can you? They have locked us in here with it, isolating its prey. We are boxed in, all of us, the lid closed and the sides taped shut. Better yet, you could even say we are now *its* Jell-O, the menu always red. It drinks us and then eats us and no one lifts a finger, not even with me screaming for any who will hear. As I have said before, this is how slick they are, how cunning and keen, running it all out in front there, just below our noses.

For the record, I hope I am loud when it comes. If I know anything about myself, I imagine I will prove to be. That is all one can ask for in this type of situation, I suppose—that in my dying I might (as Emil did for me) wake and enlighten another as to what is really going on here. Perhaps in doing so, he or she will then take up the fight as I took up the fight. Unlike me, perhaps even he or she might prevail.

OF SCAMPS AND SCUM

Goddamn you people learn hard. I mean, what part of what I've been saying don't you understand? It boggles the fucking mind.

Learning hard it is, then. I mean, it ain't like we don't have the time.

So let's see, how many is it we have here with us to-day? Little hint: I pre-counted. Means forty-seven is the number. Forty-seven pieces of shit that just refuse to learn. And yes-oh-yes, today is a day of firsts! We have our first female among us this morning. Alice Monroe is her name. Down there in the back is where you can find her, second chair from the left on the end. I reckon most of you already found her, of course, you buncha looky-loos yous, but what should really be giving you pause is the fact that you're able to hear each of them this time around. Not enough to interfere with the lesson when it begins, but enough to give each of you the nightmares you deserve.

I can't even take credit for this particular event, either,

the powers that be, the ones who thought this bad boy up. You do remember my employers, don't you? The faceless entity that has almost as much money as you? Some felt the duct tape I'm partial to applying was somewhat hindering to parts of the point we are trying to make. I can see this, I can, but what I'm enjoying most is the venue change. I mean, the foliage alone, and that we are able to roam free, our inner beasts at one with...

Yeah, I've been known to get a wee bit carried away at times. I admit that, especially when dealing with cunts the likes of you. It's why most of you will understand the importance of the wildlife preserve before us and why your cohorts sit naked and strapped to chairs in the middle of it. Brilliant, I know. Circle of life. Simba. All that shit. Brings my employers into a different shade of light is what it does, showing you it's not only money they possess. Speaks of influence, of power, but most of all, it declares a sense of irony I'm sure you'll appreciate once you've met our special guests.

Wait for it. Wait for it.

And look at this, pretty much right on cue. Before we take in the animal though, have a gander at the bald dude in front of the rest of the pedophiles down there. He look a bit different to you? All me, baby! Ha! Two pounds of ground chuck into every crook and crevice he owns. Little bit of steak sauce on top, as well, and bam! justice will have never tasted so fine.

And just look how it pounces! I mean, it's like Freddy meeting Jason down there. And listen to that! Hell, listen to them all. This is what you have to look forward to. Each and every one of you pieces of shit.

Oh, now. Would you look at this. A cub is venturing

out to be with its mother. Too cute. L'il Scamp, I'll call him. Hey, don't go too far with that intestine little guy...oops...yep, that's a little too far. Rip at it. Come on. Tug. There you go. Your very own piece of the pie. Good for l'il Scamp. Good for him.

Do we need to continue?

Of course the answer is yes. But not as we have. Not like this. What happens now is this recording will become a supercut, showcasing only the best of what this buffet has to offer. Might take hours. Might take days. You will be given the contents, regardless. Study them. Anticipate them. They will be the last of these recordings the remainder of you see. Why? Because it's not only that you fuckers learn hard but that you fail to learn at all. It proves you are more than arrogant and beyond what the world perceives as evil.

It also proves we were never really asking. Not as you thought; this whole exercise was only ever about getting us to a place where the remaining 6,479 of you would never see us coming. It won't be pretty, either, what comes next. And the hole we dig, it's gonna have to be some kind of big. But it's a thing that's needed, maybe the only thing, and as you can plainly see I am only too happy to oblige.

You see what it is I'm saying here?

If not, little hint: it's here we suggest you run.

NEW EQUIPMENT

"It breaks my heart is what it does. Because of this, I think it's fair I keep this little sermon short."

Under overhead lights, upon stainless steel tables, my words bring tears, convulsions, and a pleading that never had to be. Lean and wiry, the man lying on my left goes by Collins. On my right, heavier, lies Jebidiah Meeks. Each is restrained. Each is intubated. The pair of them as far from inheriting the earth as they were from believing in the Saviour above.

"What you boys took from me wasn't just an integral part to my life, but an investment that was years in the making." Big bills by the time everything was said and done. This included pre-op, post-op, and the actual re-construction phase being a two-part process. Two-and-a-half years later and my brother had become my sister, requisite D-cups and all. "It means you two pieces of garbage owe me not just for taking Kevin's life but for the eighty-six grand you used your dicks to destroy."

I look to their penises. Lost in a tangle of pubes, I assume Meeks is the guy who did the least amount of damage. Not that being small would save him.

"For truth, Kevin was never comfortable in his skin from the get-go. And maybe I never came to appreciate my brother's situation as maybe I should have, but I never turned my back on him, either." True, I could never fully comprehend what Kevin was going through. What I could do, however, was respect his decisions as any brother should.

"And the courage it takes for a man to transition in the world of today. I mean, I hate to say it, but the balls on that guy..."

They would never understand this, though, not without help. Each being the kind of man who takes what he wants and consequences be damned. It's why we were where we were and why the type of surgeons behind me no longer had letters trailing their names. "Brings us to the main event, once you've been put under and once you've been shaved. As it should, it will be in honor of the woman each of you raped and left to bleed out behind a dumpster last New Year's Eve. Smart guys like you, you've probably already guessed what it is though, right?"

More tears now. Followed by shakes and a style of vein reserved for heavy lifting.

I step closer, reach out, and from each of them I take a hand into my own. "My brother, all his life, he always said he felt he was something he was not. This here, forging new equipment from old, it will ensure you come to understand it as well."

A little extreme, sure, and somewhat in reverse, but dick or no dick, Kevin deserved no less.

STEPS

Her name was Carol, the love of my life. Or so I had thought.

We'd met years ago, before I got sober. Young, her face had shone fresh, but the goggles I wore were thick back then, stained with ale. Sober, she looked quite different, but I have never been one to complain—I myself nowhere near the desired type, my face a hammer, all hooks and claws. Despite this, Carol loved me. For a little while, at least.

"You going out again?" I asked, and this was the instant I knew—the beginning, as it were.

"You going to *take* me out?" Carol shot back, assuming the stance: hand on hip. She was all dolled up, more so than usual, her application of makeup thicker, fuller, like war paint gone mad. Either way, it was what it was— the man before her standing still, background to a relationship long past gone.

"No. Just wondering," I lied as the realization of the thing bloomed within my mind. "Got work tomorrow,

147

anyway. Early."

"Same old Carl," she said. And was that pity in her voice, or disdain? I can never differentiate between the two. Door closing behind her, I rose, suddenly feeling more alive than I had in years. Was it fear? Fear of knowing? Of being right? Or only that this was something new? I didn't know, not yet, but believed it to be a combination of the thoughts tumbling through my mind. How long had I been asleep? I'm speaking figuratively, of course, not literally. And this here, the question, this is what I asked myself as the days chugged on.

I was appalled, dejected, two emotions that should never be combined. They mixed though, and once they did, they became what led me on. I followed her, night after night, on the nights she went out. She hit the bars, the ones I used to frequent before I started the steps, where I had originally met her. I watched through windows out front, from the streets across the way. I also watched from out back, in alleys, where I found her on her knees.

My heart broke at this, shattered, and not for the first time. But the heart is a many splendored thing—isn't that how the song goes? It is as well a beast, and I want that known. The things I did to Carol—they are things I have come to fear. Unspeakable, they plague me, burrowing deep into what now makes me whole.

Make a decision to turn our will and our lives over to the care of God as we understand him. This is step three. Do I believe it? I want to say yes, that I believed it up until the moment my eyes were opened as to what Carol had become. Did it piss me off? Damn right it did, chafing me something fierce! Because if there were a god—

148

and I'm just spit-balling here—would he grant me the power to beat one of the worst demons known to man only to replace it with another, meaner shade of green? I mean, it's kinda wonky, even in my book.

Whatever; I have granted myself the power.

Deciding finally to confront her, I waited for her, a beer in each hand. I was not yet drunk, but well on my way. *Could there be an explanation,* I remember thinking. I wasn't sure, didn't know whether I wanted to know. And I couldn't shake the vision, either, not for a minute. Over and over I saw what I didn't want to see— Carol on her knees, her mouth full, hands sliding up and down thighs. I wanted to scream, did scream, and then I screamed again. I cried, too, there in my chair as I awaited her return. What would she say? What *could* she say? I thought of the scenario, predicted her rebuttal. She would deny it at first, as was her usual M.O. In time she would relent, and then I would finally know. But why? This was the question, the one I could not answer as I imagined her before me. She would become disgusted, and she would use that disgust—of this I was sure. She was not the woman I had married, no longer the Carol of my past. Did the fault lie with me alone? No, it didn't, but I didn't understand that at the time.

At first, I blamed myself for what *I* had become. I was sober now, normal, and the furthest thing from fun. Again, my fault? In a way, yes, but a man can only admit so much before realizing he isn't alone in the room. I had been dying, you see, my addiction full-blown. But I had been a fun drunk, a people's drunk. And the fact that I wasn't that fun person anymore—that became the problem. Finally done with alcohol, I saved myself, but I won't be boring you with every single step in the process. Carol *was* there, however, for *every* step, and this is something I think you should know. Makes what I'm about to tell you a little easier to digest, maybe. It still hurts me, though, thinking about her betrayal, especially after she stood by my side the way she did. It almost makes me wish I hadn't killed her—almost.

So sitting there in my chair, waiting to confront her, I hear her footsteps on the stairs as she approaches our second-floor apartment. Each step is thick, like trunks uprooted. Inside, she notices me right away. The look was there, as well, just as I had expected.

"Well lookie at this," she says, as she sets down her purse, removes her shoes. "What the fuck are you celebratin'?" And that was when I knew she no longer loved me. Hell, she probably didn't even like me by this point.

"Nine years," I say, and my speech is slightly slurred. "Nine years and this is all that you can think to say?" Did I expect indignation? Sure, maybe. But I expected denial as well, as I think I've already said. You know what I got? I got the truth, wanted or not.

She started by telling me I knew what she was doing and that I had known for a good long while. Fucking pansy, she called me, saying it'd be a night darker than this when I took my balls from her purse. And you know what? She was right. I had failed to keep the fun part of me alive, I guess—the part that had drawn Carol to me from the start. Is that fair? No, but it's all the woman gave me.

"And you know *why* I suck their dicks?" Seriously. In all your life would you have ever thought you would hear those words spoken out loud? Me neither. But the smirk that accompanied the question was something else entirely: pure malice. She was enjoying this. "Look at you. You've gained what, seventy, eighty pounds since we've been together? Can you even *locate* your cock?" I took aim, ready to speak, but she cut me off. "And the last time *we* fucked? When was that exactly? Can you even remember, Carl?" I didn't know what to say, suddenly realizing she was holding all the cards, or at least she was making me feel that way. My fault, she yelled, every last thing—and then what was I going to do about it. She sneered as she said these things, a viper in her pit, and it is in this moment that I feel like killing her. Not that I had planned to, not then, but murder happens fast.

She continued berating me, her voice rising as her insults escalated. "You're not a man, Carl. You know that, right? A man can at least reach the back of my throat." And that's what did it. I'm not proud about it, no, but it's there all the same: penis envy. Is there anything crueler than that to a man? Probably. I lack the necessary vocabulary to give you a name, however. And I know what you're thinking: why would someone admit to such a thing, 'specially a man? Step 12, buddy, step 12: honesty in all things. Might not mean much to you, but dude, it is everything to me.

I stood up as she went on, her mouth just running, sucking in air. She never let up, never moved back. I hit her middle of the chest, giving her everything I had. I can't say for sure that I stopped her heart with that first punch, but I did stop her mouth. On the ground now, I straddled her, ensuring my hands received all the room they would need. I believe *Die, woman, die,* might have escaped my lips. If not, no matter, because it sits there now. Everything I've said—it will all be admissible, yes? Good. Good. It needs to be known, the kind of woman she was, the kind of man she made me become. I blame her fully, yes, but can't help thinking she was right and that this is why she came to resent me so. I am an addict, as I said, and have been my entire adult life. I beat alcohol, beat it hard into the ground. But unaware at the time, I also traded one addiction for another, and this is what I think Carol was trying to say—that mediocrity is far from worth even part of the trade. And that possibly, for whatever reason, I should have remained a drunk. Who knows, though, right? I mean, seriously, the woman had issues.

You, ah—you think I could get that cuppa coffee now?

NEW CORPORATE MANDATE
A Bishop Rider Story

You like stories, Joel? I like stories. Each one holds all the ingredients this world needs to propel itself on. There are good stories. There are bad stories. Stories so fucked up you can do nothing but hang your head in dismay.

These are the kinds of stories I wish to discuss.

They involve good guys and bad guys and people just ignorant enough to believe they are beyond reproach. Granted, I was late to the game, Joel, but just so you know, Bishop Rider is the guy I've come to put my money on. The name rings a bell, I see. Good. I'd want it no other way.

Long story short, I wasn't there when the Abrum brothers ripped Bishop Rider's life apart. I enter the frame years later and bear witness as he takes down the younger brother down. He is like a machine when he does this, and my mouth gapes like a cave as I watch a man's face trade places with his throat.

Hit the fast-forward button, and Rider and a man named John Batista intercept the older Abrum, reducing him to what I've been told were the roughest cuts of beef. Nevertheless, the job they began together was far from over. Batista and Rider enlist me, my connections to people far worse than I being my ticket onto the team.

We continue on, the three of us, cleaning up as many participants connected to April and Maggie Rider's deaths as we can. After that, we go further still, accumulating years and bodies in between, doing things I can honestly say I would do again.

Wasn't until Mapone entered the picture that circumstances changed.

Rider's mistake was letting the big man live; he'd wanted Mapone to stand as a walking, talking example to all who would choose to make a living the way Mapone did. It worked, too, but only for a while. Eventually Mapone came back on Rider with a vengeance. Mapone hires neo-Nazis to take Rider out, and they capture him and tie him to a chair.

This is where it happens, Joel. Where Rider should have been killed. This does not occur, not as it should. Instead, a man by the name of Jeramiah steps in and saves Rider's life. Rider ends up a tad lighter than he had been that morning—yes, by half a leg, in fact; but hey, he'd still be granted the right to fight another day.

The last name of the man who changed the outcome of that day?

Abrum, baby. *Abrum.*

Twenty years removed, the son of the man who'd killed Rider's sister and mother is the man who pulls Rider from the flames. What would one call such a development, Joel? Ironic, maybe? Just? Coincidence or fate? Whatever it's called, it's accepted, and Jeramiah Abrum is brought into the fold, his role becoming that of bene-factor, and only because he has almost as much money as you.

Now this brings us to the second story I wish to discuss today. For truth, it intersects with the story you just heard, story one, but this story, story two, will have a much different outcome. For starters, with regard to these other men sitting beside you, just the amount of bodies alone is going to become a thing unto itself. We warned you, too, all of you. But even that did not deter you from making the movies we told you to stop making. We have burned you. We have buried you. We even have that time we took a few of you out to a nature preserve and let the animals have their way with you.

Speaking of animals. Let's get a closer look at the men here with us today. Not only do we have an educator is our midst, but a banker, as well. Beside him is our model, now suspiciously down quite a few teeth. Rounding out the line is a stay-at-home dad and a doctor, of all things.

It proves you just don't get it, Joel. None of you do. It's why men like us insert ourselves into situations such as this, and why you should fear us. It's why, like Rider and the axe that maimed him, each of you will be leaving lighter than *you* arrived.

Unlike the axe thrown at Rider, though, the arc I create will be travelling a little farther north.

MAKING SPIRITS BRIGHT

By the time he starts in on the second cake, I can't help but be impressed. His footwear erases this: black boots, not dirty sneakers, the finishing touch to every Santa suit the world over.

"Remember what I said, though, take them as you find them, pubes, piss, and all. You keep that in mind, you just might get outta here alive." He looks up at me from his position on the tiled floor, blue pieces of crust caught and holding in his not-so-jolly beard. He grumbles something, a thank-you I think, and then his hands dip into the middle urinal, the one that held most of his blood.

Six days late with his second payment, he deserved more than the beating he'd already taken. It was Christmas, though, and this time of year has always held a special place in my heart. Might bring me some heat, not doing Lionel as I should. And let's be honest, I'd probably be taking care of him before this time next week, but Santa costume or not, things remain as I like them, this time of year bringing out nothing but the best in me.

"That's it, m'man. Keep it goin'. Like I said: you do all five cakes, I let you walk. Do not confuse this with a free pass though. You're still gonna owe." Would he pay? Does Trump have big hands? He'd tell himself he'd pay, sure, as this is what men like Lionel do. What most of his kind fail to realize is there's really no need for men like Marcus to employ men like me. It doesn't bother me, not like you'd think, as I appreciate consequence for the engine that it is.

Some would disagree with my thought process here, but seeing as I once stopped a man who used intestines for tinsel, I'll stick with my way of thinking, thank you very much.

"You're not slowin' down on me here, are you, partner? Be quite a shame if you start doin' such a thing, seein' as far in as you are." The fat man shakes his head, doubles down, but yeah, a little bit of "making room for seconds" has gone and entered the equation.

The guy using innards as ornaments was a disgruntled employee from back in the day. The piece of garbage decided that Marcus's son was the one and only way to go about voicing his displeasure. What we ended up doing to that man in response (think man-puree, but chunkier) is the reason I do what I do now. We all need hope this time of year. We all need spirit. We become savages otherwise.

"Maybe think of it this way: imagine how fresh your breath is bound to be come New Year's. You start concentrating on that, I'm pretty sure you'll be able to go and get that last one down."

Pulling himself down the line of urinals, he reaches in and grabs the last puck. It's full and brand-new, and the look it creates on his face runs counter to the one spreading across mine. Done, he fails to void, and I'm amazed at the turn of events. I was sure of the addendum about to come. Instead, I slip from my position between the sinks and offer him my hand. He's wary, of course, and I can understand why.

I tell him not to worry, not for the immediate future, anyway. He has done what I have asked, the pair of us committing to the season and all I believe it holds.

I unlock the door and open it. The Mall's version of "Jingle Bells" is long gone and replaced by what I assume is "Little Drummer Boy." We regard each other in the archway as he takes his Santa hat from my hand, and I pat him on his way. He cringes at my touch but I understand his reaction.

It allows me to shove instinct aside and block the due diligence struggling to rise; how feeding Lionel porcelain until the hand dryers hold portions of his teeth remained a thing which wanted to be. Some would judge this as being weak and perhaps this is the case. I don't see things this way, though. Not since I was paid to turn a man to soup.

All told, it means there might be hope for me yet.

All told, it's why I love this time of year.

VANITY: NOT JUST FOR HUMANS ANYMORE

Leaving the coffee shop through the right side of the establishment's two main doors, Martin says, "Subject has been tagged. I repeat: Subject has been tagged." But what he is thinking is something altogether different: *Come on, Big Boy, don't let me down—time for you to step up and shine.*

Barlow did not stand when the human offered his hand. He felt it was beneath him to do so, even though he continued to play with his prey. A funny little man, he thought, as he watched the human scratch behind its right ear as it exited the coffee shop. Perhaps weird would be a better description, he decided. Because, really, what *was* that about?

In all his years Barlow had never had such an encounter—the human as different as different could get. Not that it mattered, not really, it just wasn't something Barlow was used to. Not a bad thing when you got down to it—just…weird, the situation not unlike the human itself.

But that was where the fun came in, wasn't it? Yes, it was. And wasn't it the entire reason he began answering the ads in the first place? Another yes, the reason for this was nothing more than tedium, boredom—that Barlow longed for something new. That wasn't entirely true, not all of it, because most of what the hunt entailed remained the same. All that had changed was the way he went about it now; he thought it might prove more intimate if he lured his prey by offering friendship before striking. In Barlow's opinion, this did something to the meat, produced a product far more tender than anything he had eaten in his three hundred years.

Center mass, he thought, his mind again turning to the human, this Martin. The more he thought about it the more he began to smile. *What the hell was that? Really, what?* For the second time he found himself wondering about the story the human had told him not minutes after they had sat down. Who does that sort of thing? A human, apparently, and Barlow again produced a smile. If anything, he had to agree with certain parts of Martin's story, especially the part about the center of a prey's chest. From experience, Barlow knew it to be where the flavor pooled, there within the heart and lungs. More than delicious, it was why evisceration had become the norm. In all honesty, it was better than cake.

And soon it would be time, he thought, finally rising to go.

Leaving, he went over all he might say to Martin tonight, perfecting the lies he would spin for the engagement at which the human wanted him to speak. Barlow chuckled at this, pleased at just how slick he had become over ther years. Why hadn't he thought of it fifty years sooner? Fifty years ago the world wasn't as it is now, not as informed. What the humans called the information superhighway was a far-off thing, yet to be developed. What people knew of werewolves came from books and movies, and plain old word-of-mouth. Nowadays everything was viral, and not a stone could be left unturned. Chat groups formed; groups became clubs. These clubs would come to have chapters, Barlow noticed. Ones like Martin's, that met the second Thursday of every second month. Barlow found that some of these chapters took out ads requesting speakers. Thinking about these meetings always made him think of cake, and then of the one and only thing that always tasted better.

"No, I really do," Barlow remarked. "With a little more polish, and once it is finished, of course, I can't see why it wouldn't be published." They sat in the front room of the house, a coffee table full of magazines and comic books between them. To his left, tight to the chair in which he sat, was an end table piled high with even more comic books and magazines. On the walls were framed pictures of dogs playing cards, and one of a bird eating what Barlow took to be a mouse. The human was disorganized, slovenly in fact—dirty glasses there, empty plates here. On the couch across from him, Martin beamed. It was a look Barlow had seen many times before on more than a few faces.

"Now I *know* you are feeding me some horseshit," Martin Udeski challenged, but only playfully so. "Another beer?"

"No, thank you. I have to drive."

"Smart man. Can't be too careful these days."

"Agreed."

"You want to run it by me then, what you're going to say?"

"That would be fine," Barlow said, thinking of where to begin. He wanted to time it just right—wanted the human at the peak of surprise. "Since your chapter isn't that big, I'd like..."

"Hold on there, Chief. What do you mean we ain't that big? Dude, we are eighteen thousand strong. Nationwide! Between you and me, I'd say that's a fair chunk a change."

"Martin. Come now. Out of fifty states? Do the math; seriously. I do not do this to poke fun. I do this because I'm a realist. Can we come to agree on that?" The stocky man looked at him, stared at him, finally smiled.

"Settle down there, partner. I'm only messing with you," Martin said and leaned forward, elbows to his knees. "I know we ain't a large group, not like some of those others. We ain't the Vampire Nation, that's for sure. The League, neither. Just a strong bunch of guys infatuated with what the werewolf might embody. Hell, some of our members actually believe in them! How's that for crazy?"

Barlow laughed, chuckled, really.

"What's so funny?" asked Martin, a crease now across his brow.

"You," Barlow answered. "And all who are like you."

"Come again?"

"Did you or did you not tell me that my appearance tomorrow night is going to be a surprise—that you and only you know I am your guest speaker?"

"So what? What's your point?"

"No point. Just playing my part in the game."

"Look, friend. Maybe I'm a little confused here..."

"Then by all means, let me shed some light. I am going to eat you, Martin. All of you. Starting with your chest and ending with your lungs." And there it was: terror. Barlow saw it in the human's face as its eyes widened. Now he needed only to change, the transformation doing what it did best: draw the fright, release the fear. Once the screaming started, he would pounce...

Funny, he thought, wondering why he had yet to register the scent.

"The sweat gland," Martin told him. "It's what you're trying to figure out, right? Why you can't smell the fear on me? It's because we're not afraid of you, Barlow. Me or my crew. In fact, I pretty much despise what you and your kind represent." Strange. The human's heartbeat remained the same. Steady. Flat. He was telling the truth. Interesting.

"I must admit, I'm intrigued," Barlow informed. "It's far from usual that a human like you appears."

"Oh, I will give you that—you have never met the likes of me."

"Quite an actor, too, I must concede." He was referring to Martin's voice and how it had changed. The human itself had changed as well, if Barlow were honest; the man-boy was no longer as self-deprecating as it once had been, and far from the bundle of wires it had appeared to be when first they met. No. The meat was proving to have layers.

"I am not a modest man, Barlow, I have been hunting

you for years."

"The advertisements in the paper—they were yours?"

"Figured a creature like you, I'd play to your vanity. Sooner or later I knew we'd catch up."

"It seems you have all the answers."

"No, Barlow. Just the ones I need."

"There are others, you know. More like me."

"A few, yes. But they're young and we know they are yours. We call you Infector Prime—Patient Zero. It also stands to reason that by killing you, your lineage ends. This was the goal. To find you: the First one. And by the way, I have to ask, what's the deal with only one name, seriously?"

"I am a trend-setter, what can I say? And long before your celebrities found it fashionable, I might add. Despite what your informants tell you, I am not the First one. Old? Yes. He who is the First? No."

"Not what the history shows."

"It would appear we've reached a stalemate, then. In a story, quite near the time a physical confrontation would ensue—when your team of men would storm the house, their entrance preceded only by their breaking down the door, each member hoping against hope to be the one to slay the beast? Is that about right? What Hollywood has ingrained?"

"Not particularly, no—planned on doing you myself." Barlow laughed at that and then lunged, his hands now claws extending for purchase. His mass doubled as he leaped, then tripled, bones breaking throughout and reforming just as quickly. Transformed, the werewolf roared and bared its natural teeth, now long and sharp.

"I will have your throat!" Barlow growled. Martin

brought out the Taser just as the werewolf slashed through his shirt and into the metal of his vest. The beast went down hard with a thud, its weight smashing the coffee table into shards. Like startled birds, comic books flew upward, along with glasses and plates.

Standing over the creature, Martin smiled, taking pleasure in the spasms that continued to wrack its frame. "That's ten thousand volts there, sport. How do you like me now?" Then, putting his hand to his ear and enabling the comm: "Subject is down! I repeat: Subject is down! I want a collar and manacles in here ASAP! I repeat: I need a collar and manacles now!"

Bending down, he spoke directly into the wolf's ear: "It ends here, Barlow, now and today. You will take no others, not one more child. I promise you, we have taken back the night."

From the floor, still in his true form, Barlow could only listen and observe—simply watch as the humans stormed forward with their metal and chains. With every hand they pressed upon him, he knew it was the beginning of an imprisonment he would be hard-pressed to escape, much less survive. They wore jackets, these men, with big yellow letters imprinted upon their backs: MEA. He didn't know what these letters stood for, but he knew they were meant for him.

Vanity, the human had said. Inside, Barlow howled.

LOVE YOU

"For better or worse. In sickness and health. This is what I remember agreeing to, Babe. You, after what I saw, you, I think, have decided to renege on this part of our union."

She looks at me from the couch. Him, too. And it's okay. I get it. I mean, if the shit is broken and it can't be fixed then what the fuck are we even doing here, right?

I can almost hear her thinking this, too, there as she shakes her head, and only because I know her as I do. Hell, once we get down to the floorboards and remove the nails, I probably know her better than I know myself.

"What I can't let go of is the blame—for what you did, Lori, and now for what you've done." Those pretty green eyes again, partially obscured by a hairstyle now only a few hours old. She leans forward and gags, but her gaze never loses what it's trying to convey. It's too late, sure, but I applaud her tenacity. Perhaps this brings me down to their level, agreed, as it *was* me on the receiving end, but it was she who initiated it. She who took me from my pants and into her mouth the night I ended up in this chair.

"I'll agree it was exciting. I can't deny you that. My mind alive with thoughts of Stephen King and John Irving as you did what you do best. Little could I know that life would come to imitate art with the help of not only a Caravan but a goddamn Prius as well."

There were fewer lockjaw and gypsy curses by the end of our thing, yes, but still, a price was paid.

"You were good at the beginning, too. Not at that, no, but at sticking by my side as a wife is meant to do. Things end though. More so, they fall apart." I stop here, pause, and wheel myself up to the shotguns angled into their mouths.

Took some doing, getting them hog-tied and leaning forward onto the barrels like that, but if I'm anything, I'm a man who's able to get things done. It brings forth gobs of saliva and I watch, entranced, as it flows from barrel to stock like colorless honey.

I go on, my words the thoughts of a person who has nothing but time to think. I tell them I should have known, there from the start, when we first hired Martel. After considering our options at the time, we had both agreed that it would be best to go with a physiotherapist strong enough to handle my frame.

"And you, Martel, you I truly thought well of. You'd just hoist me up, rub me down, and your enthusiasm about building up my arms was more contagious than I wanted to let on." I pat his head here, rub it. Only when he begins to vomit down the steel do I understand that my anger has gotten away from me. I turn, roll forward, and allow the man to continue as best he can.

"What I remember most, I suppose, is when it became clear that I had lost you. Not physically, but mentally. We were in Bradbury's office, there when he told us my equipment south of the equator had a less than one percent chance of ever working again."

She's crying full-on now and the tears are as fat as they are prolific. I imagine they contain regret for all the things she wishes she could erase.

I imagine she wishes I'd died.

"Wasn't until last week that everything fell into place, though. As is your way, Lori, you did this in style. The question that lingers is: did you *know* I could see what you'd chosen to do?"

I don't hold back, not being so close to the end. I tell her how slowly she went to her knees, how slowly she took him into her throat. She shakes her head at this. Martel, too. I tell them both to suck it up, the pun certainly more than intended.

"I think it was my wheels that gave me away. They aren't the quietest, I know. But sometimes it's the angle of the mirror that I recall. The very mirror in which I have watched you redouble your efforts whenever I told you I was close. And this, right here, I think this is what did it, Babe—you doing him the same way you have always done me. Seems a logical step to make. But I don't know. Not for sure. Either way, what we are is finished. What we were. And that is something I do know."

I bring out my own gun, a sawed-off, and run it down the sides of my face as I have so many times before.

I place the gun in my lap, roll forward, and reach down to pull Martel's trigger first. I look up into Lori's eyes as I do this to make sure we are finally seeing eye to

eye. She is the opposite of what marriage is—my father
and her mother all rolled into one.

For better or worse, I repeat.

For better or goddamn worse.

DIFFERENT KINDS OF TRUTH

Why doesn't he continue to run? I'm sure there are many reasons. Misinformation being the one I've come to rest my hat on. All told, you'd think having a brother done in by a snake and a father killed by a knife would be enough for a man to get himself gone, right? Not Randy. No, sir. The man decided instead to dig in and come at me hard.

Thing of it is, Randy's father remains at the root of all of this; he was the one who put a hit out on me and caused this whole situation. Another factor was the men Maurice employs and their failure to complete the job they were paid to do. Shoddy. Every part. And it begets his death, regardless. But Randy, the only remaining son, he doesn't think along such lines. Nah, he'd rather come after me, along with three other men. But like most hotheads, they're as noisy as the tricked-out Ford they drive up in.

Getting out of the vehicle they're even louder, all up and down about how they're coming for me and that hell is coming with them.

Please.

But that's the way it is with kids today. All id and ego and ice my fucking knee. Almost has me tearing up as I shoot the one with the mullet right in his eye. Down on his back like a sack of hammers he goes, the ejecta from the hole like lava as the other three dart their separate ways. One wears a John Deere hat, the other a red plaid coat. As my own Daddy used to say, fish in barrels and death on Sunday, it's all how you choose to believe in God. Agree or disagree, it's not the point. Livin' is.

I pick off two more easily, the back of their heads a couple of moons sprouting stubble through the eye of the scope. I catch sight of a buck, as well, the truck and reports having scared it out of the woods and then right back in as it realizes its mistake. Randy eludes me, though, the big man much faster than I would have believed.

Behind me, the water remains calm, lazily reflecting the sun. I take a moment. I breathe.

It was gonna be one of those days.

Milligan said if I could see my way to breaking junior's shoulders before I put him behind the glass the odds of the snake ingesting a man whole went and tripled.

I sit. I wait. I watch.

Maurice screams the entire twelve minutes it takes for this to occur.

Once it's over, once his first-born son has been devoured by a python, I take a knife to Maurice's chest and slide what remains of my fingers along the reality of my scars. They make up the majority of my scalp now, running from one non-existent ear to the other like bubbled lattice. It happened years ago, when Maurice first put the hit out. The bullet that was meant to penetrate my skull rode my head instead. His men buried me, too, just not very well, nor very deep. After I healed, I dream up scenarios and plans, recalling an incident when Maurice had confessed his greatest fear—not the smartest thing for a man in his position. At the time I said nothing, choosing instead to squirrel the info away. Little did I know I would come to use it. Or that it would bring the amount of pleasure that it did.

Revenge finally extracted, my life continues, and I decide it's time to come home. I purchase three acres along the Grand, just up from Brock, and move into a two-story cabin. I'd just begun to gut the place when the stuff with Randy began. Little things at first, the odd slashed tire here, the pile of human feces on the hood of my car there. Things escalate quickly, however, turning bright red as of this morning. He has no proof that it was me who did his brother and father, just speculation. Granted, I didn't make it any easier on myself moving back here like I did, but Culver is my home, too—long before I ever started working for Maurice.

Things are what they are, though. And like anyone, I'm unable to take any of it back. My only mistake being maybe I picked the wrong son to exact my revenge.

Yeah, maybe it was that.

He inherited it all. The cars. The house. The business.

Randy stayed away from all of them. I was there when he was born. I was there as he grew up. He'd hole up at the pool house, far at the back of the estate. It's what Alphas like him did when you had them on the run. He'd regroup, sure, as this is also what Alphas are known for, but the one thing Randy couldn't count on was me giving him the time.

"Where I can see them, son. Don't make me drop you before we even have a chance to discuss this." His instinct is to bolt, the back of his frame bracing for departure as I enter the room. As he slowly turns his head, I decide to make it easy for us both: I knock him to the ground via the metal in my hand in a one-two count.

Later, awake, he struggles against his bonds but shows some smarts and quits a few seconds in. "We're going to talk now, Randy, like both of us are rational human beings and not a couple of mutts. I'm going to tell you things you have no knowledge of. You will either accept this and understand, or object and continue to believe you are righteous in what you're attempting. Let's talk about your mom."

His eyes light up at that, there under his bangs. Sweat runs off him, soaking the undershirt he'd stripped to. But the mention of Janice, it changes the mood, heating the situation further. "What does she have to do with this?" Angry. Defiant. Everything his father had been but more. Yeah, no doubt about it: I'd picked the wrong fucking kid.

I explain how his mother and I started up a good year after Janice and his father divorced. We kept it as quiet as we could, I tell him, but even that wasn't good enough for Maurice. "He's the reason your mother is dead, Randy. The accident, it wasn't an accident. Your father was a man who was more selfish than any of us knew."

"And my brother?" What could I say? I tell him the truth.

"A man tries to kill you, it takes something from you. What this is I can't quite say, but it leaves behind a hole in need of filling. Some people have the goods to get on with it. Others, not so much; they spend their entire lives fixated on regret." He doesn't say anything, and he doesn't drop his gaze, which tells me more than a lot—it tells me everything.

"So—" but I don't allow him to finish. I can't. The look in his eyes tells me he'll never see things from my point of view. I'd like to think that if I had stayed longer or tried harder we could have come to an understanding. Wishful thinking, this, and far from what keeps you above ground in a business like mine.

I go on and do what needs to be done, finishing it. The pig-knife is the same blade I pushed into his father. As his eyes go dark and the blood comes up, I come to believe I can live in that silence forever. Not because I'm better than any of the men who've tried to kill me, but because they made me less.

For lack of a better word: my kind of truth.

ADOPTING HEALTHIER HABITS

For the second time in my life I tell my therapist it's been difficult. The transition into what I've become more challenging than I ever thought possible. However, it's the realization that I never once foresaw the outcome that really gets me going.

"Portion control, Mr. Richards. This is what's key." I could not disagree.

For years I blamed the Asians for my condition—what they represented to a mind bereft of clarity. And yes, deep down I knew it to be improper—that society viewed me as a monster. In addition, it might have been some kind of psychosomatic thing that had its hooks in me. I am willing to entertain as much. If I do, then I must also admit the link this provides to the larger problems in my life. In truth, it's the entire reason I'd sought out Dr. Bashir.

"Do you believe you are a chronic overeater? Perhaps a secret one, as well?" The man could certainly push buttons. I'm not saying I liked this about Dr. Bashir, I'm just stating a fact. Before I answer, I show him my teeth, each of them small, all of them rowed. I do this because I want to, because a man like me can. "All of the above, Doctor, as you well know. It causes me to blame others for my faults. The very reason I continue to believe myself hungry whenever I choose to eat Chinese. Before them, it was the colored man I was addicted to, and no, dear Doctor, none of my closest friends are black." When he doesn't respond, I smile again, trying my best to inform him of what I was attempting—if anything, I am an equal opportunist, not a racist.

"Speaking of black men—why do you think you desired them so?" Button Pusher. Segue Owner. But I cannot fault the man in front of me for such questions. His glasses halfway down a blackhead-encrusted nose, he waits as I take my time, and he grows more uncomfortable the longer I withhold my response. He knows what I am doing, sure, the degrees upon his wall tell me as much. Granted, he has other things occupying his mind—things that might involve me, the killing of me, and the new trajectory his life has taken. All told, it's how an apex predator like me might begin to spread his wings.

"Dark meat, Doctor—it holds the highest ratio of fat content there is. On the flipside, it's why I've chosen to give it up, as well." Don't get me wrong—I'm aware of the negative light in which I place myself by stating such things. I cannot go back, though, only forward, certain that this is the only way to get to the root of what I've let myself become. It's here that I ask the doctor if he agrees.

"Yes. But perhaps we would be better served if you explained your reasoning." Is it any wonder I chose this man to be my therapist? If I were to find balance at the end of this, more than ever I was sure it was he who could guide me there. "Because I'm tired of second-hand kills, of ordering thighs online." Which, whether I liked it or not, was probably the most honest answer I had given since these sessions began.

"And acquiring things this way—this makes you feel both weak and less than what you know you're supposed to be?" The man was brilliant, spot-on, and I took the time to tell him so. I told him that yes, I remembered this early part of my life quite well, a time when it was only about the hunt. Once I'd given myself that first taste—well, this was the crux of it, no? Clarity and ownership and bears, oh my!

I tell him yes. Yes. A thousand times yes. I am powerless over food—that my life has become unmanageable because of it. That here, now, I am seeking professional help the only way a three-hundred-and-twenty-seven-pound man like me can. Done now, I tell him the plan I have come up with, something I believe he would endorse. To start, I would be eliminating what I cherish most: the skin. Every visible trace of the outer layer removed from what would become only the leanest cuts of meat. Dr. Bashir looks up at me then, his eyes following the slope of his nose. We stare at each other, one second, two, and for a moment I sense he might bolt. This changes when I tell him the reasoning behind my plan.

"First is because of the white man himself—that he is in abundance. Second brings its own logic to the table, once you really examine the options left open to someone as overweight as I. All told, I believe it shows how committed I am to this process—that I am now willing to become the very thing I eat." His face is exactly as I had hoped it would be. Not too dark, nor too light—just the perfect shade of a man realizing he's taken on more than he can chew. As with the hunt, it is a response I have come to dream of, days of a life I am fighting to restore.

Upset, the doctor shifts, left leg now over his right. Good, as today's agenda had been twofold. Lowering my octave, I inform Dr. Bashir that I wish to speak openly to him now. What I convey is that I mean him no harm—that he is safe from me and how I live. "Besides, Indian food has never really agreed with me."

It's when his throat gives an audible click that I choose to continue.

I speak of the nutritionist he'd set me up with, remarking on how dissimilar he was from the personal trainer from a few weeks back—far more tender-looking. Getting up to leave, I reiterate that he is right: change is a process, not an event. It's as we make our way to the door that I reinforce what I must, adding that even though we'd already come to terms with regard to doctor/patient confidentiality, he still resembles a man who may or may not love his family as much as he thought he did.

Not the most subtle of performances, no, but then again, I'm a man attempting to change.

TANKED

My father stares at me, bubbles rising from his nose. I tap the glass and conclude that the soul must exist once the body has died. His head sits there, his thick black hair momentarily waving in response to my tap upon the tank. His eyes are open and they freak me out, so much so that I turn to my wife.

"Can we do it doggy-style? Him looking at us is starting to get to me."

Sure, she says, and we finish in-between the coffee table and the couch.

My mother is the one who wanted my father in the fish tank. Said a prick like him deserved no better. He can sleep with the fishes, she'd said, and then laughed that queer laugh of hers, always too high, always too long. Poor soul, my mom; even in her dreams her dreams won't come true.

"Why doesn't he decompose?" In all fairness, it was a relevant question.

"I don't know. Maybe evil is beyond destroying." Sarah looks at me from the counter, comes over and pours me another cup of coffee.

"Do you think he still sees?" And that was how my wife and I started fucking in a room that now holds the head of a man who'd ruled in absolutes. Sarah—she is the craziest woman I know. Not insane crazy, just, you know, a little weirder than most. She knows about my father, his organization, and the way I'd been raised. This doesn't bother her, not in the least. Most times this makes me smile. Sometimes, though—sometimes we all need a little alone time to let out the air.

You gonna mind me, boy. It wasn't a question, not really, but it made its way into my thoughts quite often. It wasn't the words that bothered me, however, it was the tone. To Anthony Carmichael, tone was everything.

I wasn't the only one who took the brunt of my namesake. I was specific, yes, but so was my mother, each of us a pet project to my father's special ways. I concede that my mother's life has been worse than mine, her going through things I will never know about—things she would choose to never tell. In my book this makes her my favorite, looney tunes or otherwise.

"Come on, let's do it right in front of him. Let's pretend he can see." So we did, there at the beginning, before we knew he was still alive, Sarah on her knees, me within her mouth. If I remember correctly, her cheek at times touched the glass. This is when I noticed the bubbles. No biggie, I thought, just leftover air. When I noticed the glare, and then the deepening of his brow...

"How?" I couldn't answer her. I thought of things though—things that go around and come around; of fathers and mothers and sons; of life and death and rage. And then I thought of the injections he'd been taking before he died. The ones he never missed. *Might be a scam, sure*, my father had said, *but what the fuck, we only live once, right? Who's it gonna hurt?*

We laughed as I remembered this, though Sarah far harder than I. Her exact words being: *wow, hypocrite much?*

And so now we sit, sometimes a cloth over the tank, sometimes not. Sometimes we feed the fish, sometimes we have to go out and buy more. I will not lie: it makes me happy either way. Happy he is unable to judge and happy I can finally make him see that he can only watch me now, at my choosing—that I am a man who is the complete and utter opposite of everything he stood for.

For so long I had sought his approval, even though he was the way he was. I often believed this made me weak, since he was the most obvious reason for my self-doubt. But we are given two parents. Most of us, anyway, and I'm supremely fortunate in that. I see that now, my mother half off her rocker notwithstanding. In truth, I'm glad he pushed her as far as he did, that finally there came a time when she could be pushed no further. I imagine it came as a complete surprise to my father that he went out the way he did, and by the same method he used when taking out rivals. That the man was made, that *we* are made, is what makes it all the sweeter.

"We can start trying to have a child now, then?" Sarah asks.

At this I realize how perfect my wife is; she's there inside my head. She smiles as I enter her, but I only see this because of the reflection from the glass. I pump. I pound. I thrust. My father watching this all from his side of the tank. Finished, I concentrate on his bubbles. That and, of course, his glare.

THE THIRD ROOM
A Bishop Rider Story

It starts with Batista. During a routine interrogation the man catching wind of something not quite right at a youth-oriented dance club. Pinks the place is called. Aside from the people running it, no one older than nineteen is permitted inside. No one under twelve. From the outside and on paper it looks legit; it's the inside somebody was having a change of heart about.

"Crybaby gives the place up before we even get to the reason he was there. On and on about his delicates. How he'd have to fucking kill himself before he was forced to swallow another man's hog. His words, Rider. Not mine."

I look up from the floor plans in front of me. Beard back from the dead, Batista runs a hand through all of it, stopping only to scratch hard at the parts of skin missing below his right ear. Lost to a madman years ago, it reminds me how lucky we've truly been.

"Your perp being so scared, is that something we should maybe take a look at then?"

"Hence, the floor plans," he says, and I almost respond by telling him his detective skills were showing—but no, levity and depravity do not mix. Not ever. Especially when children are involved.

People—they were about to burn.

The young man afraid of his throat being filled is Rennie Lamont. Pinched on a dime-bag, he's the type of perp who only needs a slap on the wrist to set him straight. You spend enough time on the job, these girls can be spotted two minutes into a proper sit-down. What separates Rennie from the pack is his vocal aversion to all things phallic—things he'd never experienced and probably only seen on TV. In minds like Rennie's, this is the shit that becomes the be-all and end-all. This is not to say that late night rendezvous do not occur behind reinforced bars.

It's why Rennie goes and spills to Batista what he refers to as the Third Room. "Took a beatdown for getting lost, the kid says. Says he was just looking for another washroom 'cause the one the public is meant to use had a line that was too damn long. Him on a ride, music in his ears, a couple of bouncers go and make death threats before knocking him out." Batista, as he's wont to do, shakes his head at this. "The little fucker then, he wakes up outside, just in time for one of our units to see him spread out on the ground. They approach and assess. Isn't until they have him turn out his pockets that the dime-bag starts all of this."

Strange, all of it. But that was Culver: pretty much rotten to the core. An eighteen-year-old put to sleep while looking to relieve himself, his fear of sucking cock opening his mouth wide. I had to agree: something was off.

What I couldn't know is what it would bring—that three days later I'd be down one finger, bleeding from my ears, and knee-deep in body parts that were not my own.

It closed at ten p.m. on weekdays. Midnight on weekends.

I wait. I watch. I see.

It angers me further, pushes me farther, and on night three I disable the security system running through the back entrance. Made of brick older than I, the dance club is actually a refurbished meat-packing plant, though updated more on the inside than on the out. At my side is the sawed-off, on my hip, a hatchet.

Through the kitchen/cloakroom I move left, left again, and then across the main dance floor. I stop at the north wall, pass both washrooms and descend the stairs. Bottom floor now, dank, with light coming out from under the farthest of three doors. Inside, it's being used as a storage room. Soft drinks. Chips. Bottles of water to the ceiling. I go left again, to the adjacent room and take the final set of stairs.

Before I even hit bottom, I hear everything I hoped I wouldn't.

On the second-to-last stair I raise the gun.

I open the door slowly, and they don't even register me, not at first. The one working the camera has his back to me. The man I would rip apart first is sodomizing a Down Syndrome boy so violently I want to turn away.

I can't, though. Not now. Not ever.

I raise the shotgun and enter the room.

* * *

Dirty mattresses line the floor. Chains sprout from the walls and hang from the ceiling. There is even a cage so impossibly small my stomach begins to churn. I take it in, all of it, and then I go to work. The blast gets the sodomizer's attention as he's pelted with brain and bone from the cameraman.

He pushes away from the boy, possibly a teenager, but I really can't tell—the boy with his hands to his ears, the boy who can do nothing but scream.

I continue forward and take aim, but the skinny piece of shit is quick and ducks just as I squeeze the trigger. He is on me in a heartbeat, his tattooed hands finding my face almost as fast as I find his dick. I yank. He folds. And then *I* am on *him*, my only mistake being a regrip upon his neck. Suddenly the side of my hand is in his mouth and then, just as suddenly, a finger is gone.

The pain is a beast, like fire, and then so am I. I am beyond myself, the rage rising like flames I have begun to breathe. I pick him up and rush him backward into the wall. He snarls, grunts *fuck you, I will fuck you, you are so fucking dead!* But I am on a mission, same as he. Neither of us would stop.

To our right is an unenclosed toilet, used and un-flushed. I take us down and land on top. We hit the toilet bowl hard and something breaks, but we are oh-so-far from done. I feed him porcelain, time after time. Eight times. Ten.

I stop when he no longer moves.

It's then I remember the boy.

He's made his way to a corner, wedged himself between the cage and the wall. Mewling, shaking, a trail of blood and shit erupting from him still. Nothing I say makes him understand. Nothing I say can take away his pain. I'm at a loss. I *am* lost.

I pick him up instead—take him to the storage room and wrap him in my coat. Back downstairs, I do the only thing I feel I can.

I take what's left of the two men apart. I ruin them.

I stack their bodies like wood.

"We have to highjack the narrative, Bishop. These men, they're bottom-feeders. It's the people above them we need to go after—show them they're not so untouchable as they think." We're in the back of a van much like an ambulance but one that the city has never stocked. Jeramiah sits across from me, my hand outstretched, both of his working on the wound. Angular face, close-cropped hair, his piece of shit father cannot stay in the past. I see too much of Marcel Abrum in his son, too many memories I can't let go. But unlike his father and I, Jeramiah and I have similar goals, and I'm sure that's the reason Batista gave him the call.

"All I'm saying, Bishop, is maybe now is the time to kick it up a notch. Maybe now is the time to try something new." He'd already saved my life once, replaced the bottom part of my right leg with a piece of prosthetic that would cause NASA officials to blush. On top of these things, he has taken it upon himself to bankroll Batista and me.

It's why I give him five more minutes.

But no, not really. It's really because of the boy. The

memory of what I had witnessed sends a line of white heat down the middle of me. I have seen heinous things, perpetrated a great many myself. Something inside that boy's eyes—like he knew something was wrong but couldn't tell what...

Jeramiah continues, laying out what he has in mind. It's a good plan, feasible, and leads me to believe he was already onto these guys long before Rennie Lamont relayed his fear to Batista in an interrogation room miles from here.

All told, it meant a war was coming.

I planned on dropping bombs.

The man behind the man was actually another man. Sullivan James Punter. A long scab of garbage living high on the east side. A silent partner of his brother-in-law's, he bought into Pinks a little more than two years ago. I don't know what angers me more, that he has kids of his own, or that he's been named coach of the year three years running.

After Punter has been questioned and released, I find him forty-eight hours later in his parking garage, suitcases already stowed. The hand is a problem, sure, barking against the glove, but I've worked with pain before. Probably will again.

Once I've taken him, in the trunk he goes, then back to a place of mine. Strung up, shirt off, he whimpers behind the gag.

I thought I would have things to say.

I thought I would take my time.

I end up doing neither, his guts between my boots faster

than you can believe. They steam and slide. They pile and unwind, reminding me why I have chosen to do this. Why it's imperative I carry on.

I continue to think of the boy.

THE SEVENTH MAN
A Bishop Rider Story

Stop me if you've heard this one before: six men in masks rape and murder April Rider the day she turns eighteen. They do this on tape. For money. For sport. All of it on the go-ahead given by a man named Marcel Abrum.

What you might not know is there was a seventh man involved.

The fabled seventh man.

In the recording, he sticks his head out of that washroom in that hotel room a grand total of two times. Two times this man is caught on tape. He is wearing the same type of balaclava as the others, but this man, he never participates. Why do you think that is, Bennet?

S'okay. I know it's a lot to take in. You just sit there and relax. Maybe pretend there's been some kind of mistake.

So Bishop Rider, he hunts down these men. Does so for years. From the Abrum brothers to the cameramen to the distributors. It's when he rounds up the men behind those masks and herds them into a hotel room much like

the one in which his sister is killed, this is when the un-
derbelly of Culver sees their problem for what it is. That
they themselves created said problem never even enters
the conversation, not once; and let's be real here, such an
admission would never be spoken aloud anyway, so we
might as well label things a wash from this point on.

Sound good? Sure it does.

Rider makes all six of these men something special:
nooses he fashions from strings of Christmas lights. These
men are then sent over the balcony of a fifth-floor room
at a Ramada Inn, the front of the hotel coming to dis-
play a kind of man-tinsel that is still talked about today.

But the seventh man...

He remained, still there inside the tape, eluding Rider.
Then I joined up. Fast forward twenty years, a man
named Mapone enters the frame. Catching Rider off
guard, Mapone gets the upper hand—due to the shenan-
igans of a piss-poor human I won't be getting in to—and
Rider loses part of a leg. The only reason he survives at
all is because of another man, Jeramiah Abrum. Does
that last name sound familiar? Yeah, thought it might.
The son of the man who ordered the deaths of Rider's
mother and sister. I mean, what are the odds, right? You
ask me, it would appear the apple-not-falling-far-from-
the-tree parable doesn't work quite so well in this particular instance.

What Jeramiah brings to the table is many-fold, but
what I'm going to discuss now are things as they directly
pertain to you.

As I've already stated, the seventh man could not be
found, as there was no way to verify who was behind the
mask. Abrum kept records—this is Marcel I'm talking

about, not his boy—and for such an evil, corrupt fuck, he ends up helping us from the grave.

It's the records his son gives us that bring us to now.

Those documents allow me to cross-reference certain employment records I was never privy to before. Can you guess what I discovered, Bennet? That a certain someone might or might not have worked at one of Marcel's strip clubs between the summer of '95 and the day Rider saws the man to pieces.

But wait, there's more.

It's where your own son enters the frame. That bar he hangs his hat at, as well. He likes his sauce, that boy, but what he enjoys more is answering questions that go a long way toward saving his life. You know what he told me he remembered? Mentioned you were pretty hinky there for a while when he was a kid—you pulling at your hair for the better part of a year, always going on about you'd have to be some kind of fool to think you wouldn't be caught.

I have to tell you: not one of your finer moments in the parenting department, Bennet. What I also have to tell you is this: we know. I know you know we know. And soon, to someone other than myself, you can try to explain your logic. Me, I think you had second thoughts way back when but found yourself between a rock and hard place with a madman looking down. It shows you might have had a little more human in you at one point in time. It's the twenty-year gap I'm not so sure about. I mean, the things you could have done to try and make amends in that amount of time…

It wouldn't have worked, of course, but if you'd tried, at least, it would have shown some type of personal growth. Not my department though, bud. Not when we get to the bottom of things. And we are at the bottom of things, Bennet. We can go no further. Before I leave, however, some advice: prepare.

The hours to come, he will make them feel like days.

TYING UP LOOSE ENDS
A Bishop Rider Story

I look down to the scar on my right hand. From the first two knuckles up top and down to my thumb it resembles a Y. As always, it brings back the memory of who was there and how it occurred. The who was April, my sister, now gone more years than she'd been allowed to live. The how was the two of us tearing apart a fort when we were kids, when I was as innocent and bright as the world we played in.

Back then, Kuwait and the time I would serve there was a far-off thing no one could yet predict. Same thing goes for my return, when I resumed my position on the force. All of this, every bit, it's all unscripted, just life as it was meant to be.

But monsters, they don't play fair, especially if they believe they are deserving.

The Abrum brothers destroyed my life as easily as they destroyed my kin. My mother, I believe, got off easy, her age playing a part in the reason that dumpster air became the last thing she ever breathed. April was less fortunate. Men hiding behind masks raped her to death and recorded it for all the world to see. *There's big money in breaking small cunts* is what Marcel Abrum said to me, there before Batista and I took him apart. Abrum billed what he did to April as an event, distributing it to customers who have yet to feel my wrath and some who already have. As I said: monsters.

Every goddamn one.

But the scar on my hand remains, no longer solitary but there all the same. I have lost flesh to this war. I have lost bone. All of it physical. All of it hell. But if it ensured our path, I would attempt all these things again. In a heartbeat. I'd even add a few things more.

It means I am not a good man. It means I have come to like what I do a little too much.

It means I am here to stay.

I know he's going to run even before he makes bail.

Obese, Carmichael Sloat has a handlebar mustache that hangs over pock-marked jowls. He is also partner and brother-in-law to one Sullivan James Punter, a man I disemboweled.

Sloat and Punter shared ownership of a dance club called Pinks. On paper it looked good, seemed to be on the up and up. This wasn't the case, though, not when you tugged at the seams.

Fetish porn. Human trafficking. Shit these dark old fucks got off on more than anything. In the basement of Pinks I find two men, a Down Syndrome boy, and a camera capturing things I wish I'd never seen. After I tear these men apart, I make the decision to go after the men behind these men—Sloat and Punter—the ones who'd given the go-ahead.

These dark old fucks.

I find Punter in his parking garage, suitcases already stowed. Sloat is another beast entirely: out of state the entire time this thing went down. Once home, he's brought in for questioning, arrested and then released on a million-dollar bond.

Men like Sloat are smarter than most, more often than not the reason they get away with things for as long as they do. The thing of it is, I fall on this side of the equation, as well, the difference being, I plan on doing this for far longer than any one of them.

It means I dig a little deeper, two days later finding what I'm looking for. It's then I take a trip.

One-armed Billy comes toward me as he always does, in woodland camo starving for a wash. He extends his hand, smiles, and I see a couple more soldiers have exited the ruins.

"Long time, Rider. Really long time." True, my last visit to his farm being one where we gave his pigs a taste of what Billy trained them to crave—a meal not found on any type of menu, save a rain forest or two. "If I remember correctly, the ladies ate well that day, not finishing until far into the night. Big fucking bastards, all three a them boys."

"Not here to reminisce, Bill. Got things I need to get done."

I explain myself, ask how long he thinks it might take him to do what I required.

"Depends," he says, the stub of his left shoulder saluting as best it could. "How much you say this piece of shit weighs again?"

The bags I leave outside the adjacent room. Once I'm inside the warehouse I remove his blindfold and the gag. He spits. Spits again. "They're fuckin retards, you fuck! You think they have clue one as to what the fuck is going on?!"

I rethink the gag. Stuff it back in hard.

I then tell him I know his secret, the shit he calls his worst fucking fear. Peanut butter comes next, up and down each side of his track suit. He sways as I do this, the chains not as taut as I'd like. I pause, readjust, and then open the second jar of Jif. Done, I grab the hockey bags, three in total. I drop them in front of Sloat, observe as he watches them pulse and bulge.

"That boy, he deserves more than this," I say. "All of them do."

I open the bags, the contents a blur of fur, each an eruption neither of us can turn from. Fifty or so rats per bag, they scurry to the outskirts of the inner walls, hug tight to the shadows they find there. Sloat's Tinder profile listed rats as his biggest fear. Rats, the fear his mind couldn't shake. By the look in his eyes, I would have to agree.

I close the man-door behind me. I don't turn out the lights. I don't just want him to feel what was going to happen.

I wanted him to see.

RUIN AND PAIN
A Bishop Rider Story

A month after Keeko Reyes rearranges my insides I'm still pissing blood.

"Might be time to change the way we go about things, Rider. Last time I checked, neither of us is getting any younger." Batista wasn't wrong, not about this. It would take some doing, sure, but if we meant to continue, it had to be done.

"First tell me about Fontane. We get him taken care of, you, me, and options can go have a nice long talk at a restaurant of your choosing. We can even do your hair." The Detective smiles at that, a surly little thing. I'd seen it before. I'd see it again. What I didn't plan on ever seeing again was a man named Fontane.

"Looks like the son believes he can continue from where the father left off," Batista says. Drug running. Extortion. A list the length of both my arms. His being here now, coming home, could only mean one thing: Time for someone else to bleed.

* * *

And bleed he did, on almost the exact spot I'd taken a five-iron to his father's inner ear.

"Wait! Just...wait." He's on his knees, his hands above him like he's holding up a piano. Built like his father, dressed like his father, his face displays the same blockish shape. "I know how you work. I heard. I give you somebody better, someone who might be into kids, you let me walk, right?" The kid was serious, too, what he was saying akin to what he believed to be a full-fledged plan.

I drop the nine-iron, move forward and put holes in his legs until he realizes the information he'd been given was wrong. No one walks. Not when kids were involved.

Not even close.

What he ultimately gives me pans out, his info leading us to a bungalow off Canal. More stone than wood, with a wide front porch, it stands in one of the safer parts of Culver. Families just above the poverty line lived here now, the ones who still believed. It's mid-October, chilly, the wind from behind kicking up like boots wrapped in gauze. I can't say this has anything to do with what I find, but I can tell you it has everything to do with how I respond.

Over a three-day period I watch one woman and four different men come and go. Another man is involved—jean jacket and tatts—but him I see only as he lets the others in through the front door. What I also see is a delivery service, Buttenham's Pizza, two out of the first three nights I keep watch. The kid who brings the pizza can't be more than twenty, the Buttenham's jacket he wears the same dried-blood color as his cap. I concentrate on him, a plan forming, as I couldn't risk going in, not without knowing all of the parties involved. Isn't until night four, when Buttenham's returns, that it slides into place.

The kid was the key.

Also, as Batista had suggested: it might be time to change the way we'd been doing things.

"Phenobarbital. Horse tranq. I'm playing kind of loose with the dosage, but sixty milligrams spread out should send these fuckers somewhere south of tomorrow afternoon." Batista hands me the powder, pauses, and then wishes me well.

"Just be ready with the van," I say, realizing more than ever that I'd gotten a very bad feeling somewhere along the way.

I dump the delivery vehicle in the river and walk the remaining three blocks. The jacket's a tight fit, same with the hat, but it would have to do. Dissolving, the phenobarbital is evenly spread over the two pizzas I carry. Once inside, depending on when and how fast they ate, I'd have access within the hour.

It's then we'd see what's up. It's then I'd decide how to proceed.

I give it another hour just to be sure.

Inside I hear nothing but a TV turned up loud. The place is immaculate, filled with high-end furniture I'd expect elsewhere. Hardwood floors and wainscoting throughout. I find jean jacket and tatts at the kitchen table, face-down in a slice of pizza. Beside him is the woman and beside her, another man.

I continue on, deeper, toward the back of the house. Downstairs now, I walk into a fully finished rec room. Foosball. Ping-Pong. Big screens. On one couch is another drugged piece of scum. To his left, on the carpet, lay shitbird number five. Farther on, I hear what I hoped I would not, the cries hitting me like cinder blocks through to the back of my gut. I pause, one second, two, and the cries become louder, adamant. Another room. And then another. This one has sex swings hanging from the ceiling and cameras on tripods positioned toward all three. At the back of this room, in rows, are three cribs and the sixth man passed out in front.

I shake my head. There is no god.

Batista hands me the bag and I hand him the infant. Two more children are passed off and he grabs me by the forearm. "Make them suffer," he says. This and nothing more.

It takes nine hours to complete, even with the bone saw. And it's all on the cameras they already had in place. I cut. I fasten. I tie off and cauterize. I also lose jean jacket and tatts in the process, nicking his femoral artery early in the reduction. Before me lay piles of arms, piles of legs. In front of these rest eyes, now more like marbles with tails than anything. Twelve of each, thirty-six in total, and infinitely dryer than when I began. Save the one I lost, the owners are naked and leaking, leaning against one another on one of the bigger couches I had brought in from the adjacent room. They weren't awake yet, but I planned on letting the cameras roll.

Someone would come soon. Either to see why no new product had come their way, or just to see what was up. It didn't matter. What did matter is what I say, there as I finish up. "Don't come back." From one monster to another the language would not get lost, not with people whose only currency is pain, their only goal, ruin.

It's why I offer them my name, why I suggest they try and find me before I found them.

I force myself to breathe.

Two months later. Christmas Eve and I move from the back page to the front page as soon as the video is leaked.

"Look how it's been cut though," Jerimiah is right. Whoever released it doctored it down to how they wanted it to appear. I do not speak in this version, not as I had when it was being taped. Gone are the cribs, as well, cropped from view. It looks exactly as it should, the impression they're going for blending with the perspective they require. The thing about perspective, though, when you pair it with the right set of eyes, not everyone blinks. Especially when most of the people in this world choose to keep their heads in the sand. "I mean, what do they gain by putting it out there like this?" Good question.

The better one being: what don't they?

I have a feeling it's an inside job, even before Jeramiah confirms the link. "Idiot used his wife's credit card to buy the cribs. Four at one time. People and their points.

Christ." Jerimiah is the flipside to his father, more light than dark, but I still have a hard time telling him I appreciate what he does. We couldn't have done half the shit we have without his intel and cash. Wasn't always this way, either, was worse, in fact, and for some reason I fought him hardest after he replaced my leg. Stupid. All of it. Batista finally persuades me with four little words: *he's not his father*. Man had me there. Still does.

"Daughter lives across town. O'Bannon and his wife the only ones who occupy the house. I suggest dosing her before you begin your talk. Good?"

It was.

They say not everyone is crooked. I believe otherwise. Wired from birth, we all lean toward what we desire most. It's how far people are willing to go to bend the rules that starts the slide. The strongest of us can recover from this, stopping well before we've reached the ledge. The ones who can't stop is where the trouble lies. Their desires turning to justification when it comes to hurting—or the possibility of hurting—others along the way.

From a sitting position in his bed Detective Sergeant Sid O'Bannon says this almost verbatim. Almost bald, nose like a blade, he keeps stealing looks at the missus, even though I have assured him of her safety.

"You think I wanted this? These men do not take no for an answer." I hated his voice. I hated his face. But what I hated more was envisioning the questions he would have had to entertain to get where he was. Courtesy of the butt end of my Glock, I share this displeasure.

"Fucking Christ! I'm talkin'! I'm sitting here and talkin'!"

"Tell me why you leaked the video."

"Scared. Pissed. Take your pick. You guys end up fighting amongst yourselves, maybe I slip through the cracks. You're a hard man to kill, Rider. An even harder one to catch." Figured it had to be someone with access on the inside. Was never going to be anything but, not with how it went down.

"I don't—" I don't care for don'ts. Never have. A little bit more steel informs him of this.

"Christ—c'mon!" And then he quiets down, resigned-like, sleeve up and under his nose to stem the flow. "They're watching me. Some are middle-eastern. More of them are white. They send me pictures of my wife and daughter every seven days, right to my phone. I told you: they are the hardest fucks I have even seen and I've seen nowhere near the top."

Bingo. Second floor. Everybody out. The downside was that O'Bannon stayed topside longer than he deserved. Didn't mean he couldn't go unscathed; a hard push down a short flight of stairs was the best I could manage. It left him as I needed him: functional. For a little while, at least. After that, who knows. Maybe I bring back a blowtorch. Maybe we begin where I left off.

Time would tell.

I choose O'Bannon's daughter. I feel she is the easier mark. Three days later I snap a hard-looking black man taking pictures of Christine O'Bannon as she exits Dal's Gym and Fitness. She's short, in sweats, her ponytail whipping as she walks. He's thick, down low, almost coiled in his seat.

When he's done, I follow him. It makes for a long day. Here and there, pickups and dropoffs. When he stops at an IHOP off the 1-5 I park beside his side of the car and await his return. When we get to it, he's difficult, like a snake sporting bones. But the element of surprise sees me through. It's only later, after the business end of a claw hammer makes its way through most of his right knee that I come to understand just how hard this man really is.

All men break though.

I bring out the sledge.

He gives me a slip number and not much more. It's enough.

The water is calm, cold, and darker than the night. The yacht is called the Rabbit Hole. Massive, it's eighty feet at least, and I hear the festivities long before I make my way back. I'd been there earlier, setting up charges, ensuring what had to be done, placing them below the water line, FRONT TOWARD ENEMY, every ten feet around the entire hull of the ship.

The night would light. Blood would rain. Flesh would burn.

I get their attention, unload the AK. Women scream, men return fire. I think: *you lay with the devil, you become the devil.* But I end it before it begins and make good on my promise, which had been omitted from the tape.

I told them not to come back. What I failed to realize was this: perhaps they never left.

Either way, this would do one of two things. I am prepared for both.

ACKNOWLEDGMENTS

As ever there are many people to acknowledge and thank for the pages you just read. Shane Johnson for one, and Terri Trimble for another, both gracious enough to edit their brother when they find the time. There is also Lance Wright and Eric and Christy Campbell at Down & Out Books for taking a chance and believing in me. As well, all the authors who took the time to check out and blurb the stories in the book you have before you. They all have busy lives and I thank them from the bottom of my heart for giving me a small part of it.

The one person I would like to center on, however, is my oldest son, Donnie. Long story short, Donnie asked the family to play ultimate Frisbee in July 2017. During this outing his father thought he could still run like a twenty-four-year-old instead of his forty-four-year-old self. Ha! Silly Daddy! Frisbees are for kids! One broken collarbone later, Donnie, of course, blamed himself for the outcome. Probably still does if I know my boy. Anyway, Donnie: not your fault. Never was. Never will be. Would have happened whether we played football or baseball or chose to knit afghans. What I mean to say is this: if I hadn't broken my collarbone this book would not have been written! And for that I will be eternally grateful. As something I thought would never happen once happened again. You were a big part of that, son. Know that. Embrace it.

Last but not least is you, dear Reader. I value you. Your time. And I thank each of you for giving me yours.

Everything else? Well, that is mine, my friends, all mistakes included.

Until I see you when I see you,

Beau
September 2018

PREVIOUS PUBLICATION CREDITS

Some of the stories in this collection have been previously published:

- ➤ "What Julie Said"—Out of the Gutter Online
- ➤ "Free Food and Bean Bags"—Shotgun Honey
- ➤ "A Patient Man"—out of the Gutter Online
- ➤ "Bipolar Bowler"—Horror Sleaze Trash
- ➤ "Father Knows Best? My Dad knew Jack"—Bartley Snopes
- ➤ "Family Meeting"—Out of the Gutter Online
- ➤ "Advice, Free or Otherwise"—Spelk
- ➤ "New Equipment"—Spelk
- ➤ "Resty Acres"—Not Your Average Monster, Volume 1, Edited by Pete Kahle
- ➤ "Making Spirits Bright"—Out of the Gutter Online
- ➤ "Vanity: Not Just for Humans Anymore"—Sein Und Werden
- ➤ "Tanked"—The Molotov Cocktail
- ➤ "Love You"—Out of the Gutter Online
- ➤ "Steps"—Horror Sleaze Trash

BEAU JOHNSON lives in Canada with his wife and three boys. He has been published before, usually on the darker side of town. Such fine establishments might include Out of the Gutter Online, Spelk Fiction, Shotgun Honey and the Molotov Cocktail. Besides writing, Beau enjoys golfing, pushing off Boats and certain Giant Tigers.

BOOKS

On the following pages are a few
more great titles from the
Down & Out Books publishing family.

For a complete list of books and to
sign up for our newsletter,
go to DownAndOutBooks.com.

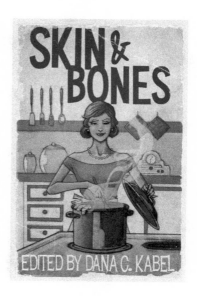

Skin & Bones
Edited by Dana C. Kabel

Down & Out Books
November 2018
978-1-948235-53-2

From a host of bestselling and award-winning authors come the stories from the darkest corners of their imaginations featuring one of the most abhorrent acts of mankind; cannibalism!

Featuring stories from Lawrence Block, Stuart Neville, Jason Starr, Dave Zeltserman, Charles Ardai, Joe Clifford, Rob Hart, Richie Narvaez, Thomas Pluck, Patricia Abbot, Terrence McCauley, Tim Hall, S.A. Solomon, Bill Crider, Angel Luis Colón, Tess Makovesky, Marietta Miles, Ryan Sayles, Liam Sweeny, Glenn Gray, and Dana C. Kabel.

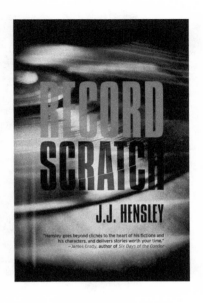

Record Scratch
A Trevor Galloway Thriller
J.J. Hensley

Down & Out Books
October 2018
978-1-948235-35-8

Somewhere there exists a vinyl record with twelve songs recorded by the legendary Jimmy Spartan. Trevor Galloway has been hired to solve Spartan's murder and recover his final songs.

When his client terminates their first meeting by taking her own life, Galloway's journey takes him into the arms of an old flame, the crosshairs of familiar enemies, and past the demons in his own mind.

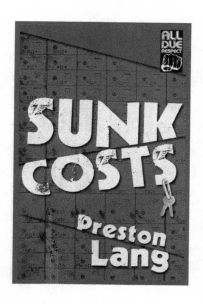

Sunk Costs
Preston Lang

All Due Respect, an imprint of
Down & Out Books
978-1-946502-88-9

Dan is a con man and drifter who thinks he just hitched a ride back east. Instead, he finds himself going 70-miles-an-hour with a gun pointed at his head. But instead of a bullet, he's hit with a proposition to make some fast money. Soon Dan finds himself deeply involved with misdirection, murder, and the sexiest accountant he's ever met.

Desperate Times Call: Stories
Hector Duarte, Jr.

Shotgun Honey, an imprint of
Down & Out Books
978-1-64396-000-5

The world can be a difficult place to navigate. Society constantly works to pull us away from what's important. We spend most of our time working for a check, that we might only enjoy 25% of. What happens when someone has enough and decides to push back? When they decide to embrace their destiny? Tragic as it may be.

How do we answer when Desperate Times Call?